Teens and Smoking

Gail Snyder

ReferencePoint
Press®

San Diego, CA

© 2016 ReferencePoint Press, Inc.
Printed in the United States

For more information, contact:
ReferencePoint Press, Inc.
PO Box 27779
San Diego, CA 92198
www.ReferencePointPress.com

LIBRARY OF CONGRESS CATALOGING-IN-PUBLICATION DATA

Synder, Gail.
    Teens and smoking / by Gail Synder.
        pages cm. -- (Teen choices)
    Audience: Grade 9 to 12.
    Includes bibliographical references and index.
    ISBN-13: 978-1-60152-918-3 (hardback)
    ISBN-10: 1-60152-918-X (hardback)
    1. Teenagers--Tobacco use--United States--Juvenile literature. 2. Smoking--United States--Juvenile literature. I. Title.
    HV5745.S976 2016
    362.29'608350973--dc23
                                                                            2015013413

Contents

A New Generation Decides About Smoking

Maggie attends high school in Coral Gables, Florida, where a lot of her friends are smokers. When they began encouraging Maggie to join them, she gave in pretty easily. Now she barely notices the warning labels on the packs of cigarettes she smokes and is certain that smoking is not going to ruin her life. "I could quit any minute," says Maggie, age sixteen. "I don't choose to."[1]

Fifteen-year-old Marissa in Virginia is solidly against smoking no matter what her peers do. She says, "In my opinion, every puff you make is a breath you'll never take."[2]

Young people like Maggie and Marissa have many important decisions to make on their way to becoming independent young adults. They will soon be deciding whether they want to go to college and what careers they want to pursue. And while they are making these decisions they may also be coping with distancing themselves from the values of their parents, dealing with their own changing bodies, and the strong need to do the things their friends do.

Whether they should smoke cigarettes or similarly dangerous products—such as flavored cigars, hookahs, or e-cigarettes— is one of the decisions they might find themselves making in their adolescent years. While health experts have for decades advised smokers of the health risks of smoking, many young people ignore that advice and choose to smoke.

Some teen smokers continue to smoke well into their adult years, but others do find ways to quit, concluding for themselves that taking up smoking was a poor decision. "I'm not proud of it now. If anything, I'm scared," says sixteen-year-old

Jerome Manansala, who gave in to peer pressure at age fourteen when he lit up his first cigarette. He adds, "I'm quitting this year. I've said it before, but I swear this time isn't just an empty promise. I know now I owe it to myself to stop, and the reasons I had for starting were just not good enough. If I could say one thing to those younger than me that are about to start smoking, I would say it just isn't worth it."[3]

Girls Under the Most Pressure

Smokers like Jerome and Marissa fell into the smoking habit because they felt pressured by their friends to smoke. While the pressures of adolescence exist for both sexes, girls can have an even tougher time navigating through their teen years than boys—and find more reasons to start smoking. Marta De Borba-Silva, a doctoral student at the Loma Linda University School of Public Health in California, outlines some of the reasons girls may be more attracted to smoking than boys:

> "If I could say one thing to those younger than me that are about to start smoking, I would say it just isn't worth it."[3]
>
> —Jerome Manansala, sixteen.

> Adolescence is a difficult time, but more so for girls than boys. Girls become sensitive and their self-confidence goes down; they may struggle with insecurity and depression—cliques, boys, looks, and weight. Our culture does not have such rigid standards of looks and weight and being "the right way" for boys. Every day, however, girls are bombarded with unrealistic images of "the ideal female" on magazine covers, television, and in the movies—our whole culture of celebrity.[4]

According to De Borba-Silva, one in four adolescent girls suffers from depression, a rate 50 percent higher than for boys. This higher rate of depression among girls can be attributed to

Some teens begin smoking because their friends encourage them to do so. Although both adolescent boys and girls experience such peer pressure, additional factors make girls more likely than boys to start smoking.

a large degree to how girls react to their changing hormones. She says smoking becomes a way to mask their angst by feeling as though they are members of a popular crowd. For example, she says, girls who fret over their weight are more likely to seek a crutch—such as smoking. "Girls preoccupied with their weight are more likely to take up smoking," she says. "Girls who diet daily are twice as likely as girls who diet less often to have tried smoking."[5]

But to students like Adam, who attends high school in Denver, Colorado, comments by experts such as De Borba-Silva are exactly what he does not want to hear. Adam says he wishes adults would stop giving antismoking lectures. He says, "I really don't care what society says about it. Smoking is a personal choice. It's not like we're hurting anybody else. It's not like we're going around in gangs and shooting people."[6]

Benefits of a Tobacco-Free Life

In fact, though, health experts have known for decades that smokers do harm to others besides themselves—many people develop respiratory illnesses or cancer when they are exposed to secondhand smoke. According to the US Centers for Disease Control and Prevention (CDC), the federal government's primary health advocacy agency, since 1964 some 2.5 million Americans have died from illnesses caused by breathing other people's cigarette smoke.

That is the type of well-established fact that has been readily available to teenagers and others for many years. In fact, young people today have more information than past generations about the link between smoking and cancer, emphysema, heart disease, and many other illnesses. Young people of past generations were even misled into believing that cigarettes were a healthy way to blow off stress and maintain a healthy weight. Unlike young people who entered their teen years a generation ago, today's teens cannot legally purchase cigarettes in convenience stores or see cigarette commercials on television. However, unlike their parents they are exposed to a new explosion of tobacco products unknown in past generations, as well as electronic devices that provide new ways to inhale the toxic vapors of tobacco.

> "I really don't care what society says about it. Smoking is a personal choice. It's not like we're hurting anybody else. It's not like we're going around in gangs and shooting people."[6]
>
> —Adam, high school student.

Today, teens still face pressure to use tobacco. Some, such as Maggie and Adam, have given in to that pressure and made the decision to smoke. But while Maggie and Adam seem to have no qualms about their new habit, Jerome has come to the conclusion that smoking is not in his best interest. That is also the decision that was made by Marissa, but unlike the others Marissa found a way to resist the pressure to smoke and now can expect to enjoy all the benefits of a tobacco-free life.

Chapter One

Who Is Smoking What?

Jasmine S. is a high-achieving teenager. She runs cross-country and is so committed to living a drug-free lifestyle that she works with middle school students to discourage them from using dangerous substances, including cigarettes. "I would never smoke cigarettes. I don't think people who smoke are attractive, and obviously the things give you cancer,"[7] the high school student says.

But Jasmine takes a more tolerant view of electronic cigarettes—also called e-cigarettes or vape pens. The devices are battery-powered nicotine delivery systems originally created as a tool for smokers to reduce their dependence on cigarettes. Jasmine discovered vaping after she spotted an attractive guy artfully curling smokelike vapor from a vape pen while she was out with her friends. She thought he looked cool.

Curious about what he was doing, Jasmine started a conversation with the young man about his e-cigarette, and he let her try it. She found the experience pleasurable. Now Jasmine and her friends use vape pens once a week when they get together. "I just use them socially because I like the taste and the feeling. I don't think it's dangerous. I definitely don't feel hooked on them,"[8] Jasmine says.

Nonsmokers Are Trying E-Cigarettes

By 2015 e-cigarettes had been available in America for about eight years. What is new about them, however, is the popularity they are gaining among young people, including those such as Jasmine, who would never consider smoking a conventional cigarette. In fact, according to a 2014 study by Monitoring the Future, a University of Michigan program that studies the habits of young people, for the first time more teens are using e-cigarettes than conventional tobacco cigarettes. The study monitored the habits of more than forty-one thousand eighth, tenth, and twelfth grade students across the country.

Moreover, the survey found that about 9 percent of eighth grade students had used an e-cigarette compared to just 4 percent who had smoked a conventional cigarette in a thirty-day period observed during the study in 2014. The numbers were higher for high school seniors: 17 percent of them had used an e-cigarette compared to 14 percent who smoked traditional cigarettes. In addition, the University of Michigan researchers also found that, just like Jasmine, up to 7 percent of e-cigarette smokers observed during the study period had never smoked a paper cigarette.

Says the Monitoring the Future study, "E-cigarettes now have the highest 30-day prevalence of all tobacco products, including regular cigarettes, at all three grade levels. . . . Substantially fewer students associate 'great risk' with using e-cigarettes regularly as compared to smoking one or more packs of cigarettes per day."[9] In each of the three grade levels that were studied, about 14 percent of the students believed their health would be at risk by smoking e-cigarettes. In contrast, 62 percent of eighth grade students, 72 percent of tenth grade students, and 78 percent of twelfth grade students recognized the dangers of smoking conventional cigarettes.

> "Substantially fewer students associate 'great risk' with using e-cigarettes regularly as compared to smoking one or more packs of cigarettes per day."[9]
>
> —Monitoring the Future study.

E-Cigarette Use Doubles

Perhaps more startling is a 2015 CDC statistic reporting that the number of middle school and high school students experimenting with e-cigarettes more than doubled in a two-year span. The

CDC report shows that e-cigarette use by middle school students jumped from 1.1 percent in 2013 to 3.9 percent in 2014 and e-cigarette use by high school students shot up from 4.5 percent in 2013 to 13.4 percent in 2014. Because the pens work without the unpleasant smell that burning tobacco gives off, teens can use them without the telltale odor of tobacco on their breath or clothes—which would alert their parents and other adults that they are using tobacco. "The increased use of e-cigarettes by teens is deeply troubling," says Thomas Frieden, director of the CDC. Frieden suggests that teens who start a smoking habit by using e-cigarettes may be prone to move on to conventional cigarettes and could find themselves addicted to nicotine. He says, "Nicotine is a highly addictive drug. Many teens who start with e-cigarettes may be condemned to struggling with a lifelong addiction to nicotine and conventional cigarettes."[10]

> "Many teens who start with e-cigarettes may be condemned to struggling with a lifelong addiction to nicotine and conventional cigarettes."[10]
>
> —Thomas Frieden, director of the CDC.

The National Institute on Drug Abuse (NIDA), an agency of the federal government, has characterized e-cigarettes as effective as conventional cigarettes in delivering nicotine to the body. The only difference, according to the agency, is that cigarettes deliver nicotine through smoke, while e-cigarettes deliver the chemical through vapor. Says the NIDA, "Because they deliver nicotine without burning tobacco, e-cigarettes appear as if they may be a safer, less toxic alternative to conventional cigarettes. Although they do not produce tobacco smoke, e-cigarettes still contain nicotine and other potentially harmful chemicals. Nicotine is a highly addictive drug."[11]

E-Cigarettes Are Fashionable

Middle school student Hannah A. says that she has seen other students take out vape pens during class. Her school is not the only one where vape pens can be found in backpacks along

with pencils and textbooks. In Santa Clara County, California, school counselor Candace Garcia has noticed more girls showing off their vape pens at school almost as if they were extensions of their clothing. "It's like you're pulling out lipstick, you want to look like you match. So with this e-cigarette or vaporizer pen, if it's hot pink and you have a hot pink purse, it looks cool. I've seen it a lot."[12]

The look is not the only attraction young people have to e-cigarettes. Taste is another feature that e-cigarette makers use to attract customers. A team of fourteen researchers at the University of California at San Diego spent two months counting the number of flavorings available to e-cigarette users in 2014. At the conclusion of the study they found that more than seventy-seven hundred different flavorings are available to e-cigarette users. Moreover, they determined that more than four hundred fifty different e-cigarette brands are available on the market.

Sharon Cummins, one of the study authors, says, "The numbers are pretty startling. How can you even come up with

Menthol Cigarettes

Menthol cigarettes, those that have an additive derived from the mint plant, are extremely popular with smokers, including teenagers. For instance, one-third of Canadian high school students who smoke favor menthol cigarettes, according to a study of more than forty-seven hundred students that was published in 2014 in the journal *Cancer Causes and Control.* The study also found that teens who smoked menthols smoked substantially more cigarettes a week (forty-three on average) than teens who smoked non-menthols (twenty-six on average per week). The author of the study, Sunday Azagba, a professor at the University of Waterloo in Ontario, Canada, says, "The appeal of menthol cigarettes among youth stems from the perception that they are less harmful than regular cigarettes. The minty taste helps mask the noxious properties, but the reality is that they are just as dangerous as any unflavored cigarette."

Menthol cigarettes are extremely popular in the United States, too, with menthols accounting for 25 percent of cigarette sales. African American smokers are especially attracted to menthols, with 85 percent of them opting for menthol cigarettes; this is three times the rate at which white smokers light up menthols. Marketing may be to blame. "We are specifically targeted by the tobacco industry to smoke them," says Delmonte Jefferson, executive director of the National African American Tobacco Prevention Network in Durham, North Carolina. However, Lorillard, a leading tobacco company based in Greensboro, North Carolina, says it does not target African Americans with its marketing.

Quoted in Robert Preidt, "Teens Who Prefer Menthols Are Heavier Smokers: Study," *HealthDay*, June 10, 2014. http://consumer.healthday.com.

Quoted in Abigail Jones, "Making Menthol Uncool," *Newsweek Global*, April 18, 2014, p. 47.

7,700 flavors?"[13] The study's authors found that e-juices, as the flavorings are called, are available in flavors that have plenty of appeal to young people. For example, e-cigarette companies have formulated flavors so the vapor tastes like gummy bears and bubble gum. Adds Richard Miech, one of the authors of the Monitoring the Future report, "E-cigarettes have made rapid inroads into the lives of American adolescents."[14]

Appeal of Flavored Cigars

E-cigarettes are not the only smoking products that have found appeal among young people, in part because of the candy-like flavorings added by the manufacturers. In recent years flavored cigars have found users among young people. The tastes and aromas of flavored cigars mimic familiar snacks such as Jolly Rancher candies and drinks such as Kool-Aid. Flavored cigars also come in chocolate, strawberry, fruit punch, and pink berry varieties that would seem as though they were concocted specifically for the tastes of young users.

According to the Campaign for Tobacco-Free Kids, every day some twenty-seven hundred adolescents will try their first cigars—and there are plenty of inexpensive cigars on the market, many of them flavored—that young people would find affordable. "The cigar market is the most heavily flavored of all tobacco products and for decades, tobacco industry internal documents have highlighted that flavors appeal to youth and young people," says Cristine Delnevo, director of the Center for Tobacco Studies at the School of Public Health at Rutgers University in New Jersey. "What we found is that the preference for flavored brands was high among females, minorities and young people."[15] When Delnevo looked at the responses of sixty-seven hundred people over the age of eleven who said they had smoked cigars in the past month, she was able to determine that 90 percent of the twelve- to seventeen-year-olds had smoked a flavored cigar.

According to the CDC, more than 40 percent of smokers in middle school and high school are fans of flavored cigars. CDC senior adviser Brian King says, "We know from the existing science that flavorings can mask the harshness and taste of tobacco, making them easier to use and more appealing, particularly for youth. The fact that these products are available is problematic."[16]

Skinny cigars sometimes look like close cousins to cigarettes that are wrapped in brown paper—in fact, another name for a tiny cigar is *cigarillo*. According to the Monitoring the Future survey, teenage boys are more likely to smoke little cigars than teenage girls—26 percent of twelfth grade boys had used them during the Monitoring the Future study period compared to 12 percent of girls in the twelfth grade. The survey's researchers did not ask eighth graders or tenth graders about their use of little cigars.

Most Young Cigar Smokers Do Not Want to Quit

According to a report from the CDC, teenage smokers of little flavored cigars are happier with their habit than adult cigar smokers. Some 60 percent of the teens admitted that they have no plans to stop smoking them anytime soon, whereas only 49 percent of adult smokers were adamant about not giving up their cigarillos.

Fifteen-year-old Andrew, however, has been smoking strawberry, raspberry, and mint chocolate–flavored cigars for five months. The tenth grade student who also smokes cigarettes believes he knows the risks. "To be honest I know they're dangerous but I'm not concerned. I don't inhale. I'm only planning to smoke for one to five years so it's not going to have a huge effect on my life,"[17] Andrew says. At a dollar apiece he can easily afford to buy flavored cigars, and if he cannot persuade store owners to sell him cigars he asks friends' older siblings or strangers to buy them for him.

"For all intents and purposes, these products are flavored cigarettes,"[18] King says. The Campaign for Tobacco-Free Kids has been even blunter in its assessment of flavored products, describing them as gimmicks tobacco companies are using to lure young people into smoking. Add the authors of the Monitoring the Future study, "A concern to the public health community is that these products will have the effect of reversing the hard won gains in reducing cigarette smoking among youth. Small cigars deliver and combust tobacco in similar ways and therefore carry similar dangers."[19]

Using Hookahs

In addition to flavored cigars, another tobacco product that is gaining favor among young people is loose tobacco smoked in a device known as a water pipe or hookah. The hookah, which originated in India, Pakistan, and countries of the Middle East, is believed to have been first used more than five hundred years ago. In recent years, though, the hookah has found a rebirth—particularly among young people. In many cities businesses known as hookah bars have opened, providing the devices for customers who must be at least eighteen years old to patronize these establishments.

Hookahs often resemble large candlesticks with long hoses attached to them. Hookahs work by heating tobacco, called *shisha*, without burning it. The heated water, laced now with chemicals given off by the heated tobacco, emits a vapor that can be inhaled. Hookah users suck in the vapors through the hoses.

The Monitoring the Future study looked at hookah use among young people and found that 23 percent of teens smoked tobacco through the devices in 2014, reflecting a rise

The number of teens smoking tobacco through water pipes known as hookahs (pictured) has risen in recent years. These devices heat tobacco without burning it, creating a vapor that the user inhales.

in recent years. In 2010 Monitoring the Future recorded hookah use at 17 percent of teens. According to the study, teenage boys are experimenting with hookahs slightly more than teenage girls—25 percent of teenage boys have used hookahs, compared to 21 percent of teenage girls. The typical teenager who has tried a hookah is a white male who lives in a big city, has college-educated parents with a high standard of living, and is also a cigarette smoker, according to Joseph Palamar, an assistant professor of population health at New York University's Langone Medical Center. He says, "Given the cost of frequenting hookah bars, it is not surprising that wealthier students, as indicated by higher weekly income, are more regular visitors, although it remains unknown what proportion of hookah use occurs in hookah bars [rather than] in homes or other non-commercial settings."[20]

No Safer than Cigarettes

Teenagers who use hookahs—which can be purchased online for as little as fifteen dollars—may believe that the practice is healthier than smoking cigarettes, but it is not. It is a common assumption, however. More than half of eighteen- to thirty-year-olds surveyed by doctoral nursing student Mary Rezk-Hanna at the University of California at Los Angeles incorrectly believed that smoke passing through the hookah's tubing had undergone a filtration process.

A pamphlet produced by the World Health Organization (WHO), the United Nations' public health arm, states,

> The illusion that water pipes are a safe form of tobacco smoking goes back at least to the 16th century, when physician Abu Fath suggested that the 'smoke should be first passed through a small receptacle of water so that it would be rendered harmless.' This early disguise of tobacco's toxicity was presumably well-intentioned, but created the illusion of safety with no evidence—then or now—of actual reduction in disease risk."[21]

Like Smoking One Hundred Cigarettes at Once

Palamar says that using a hookah, which can last as long as two hours, is far more harmful than smoking a single cigarette, which burns down in a few minutes. The WHO has described a single hookah session as the equivalent of inhaling one hundred or more cigarettes. Still, Palamar thinks that most teenagers who indulge in hookah use do so only occasionally and would not react well to scare tactics from adults. "Saying, 'If you do this once with your friends, you'll get addicted and get cancer' is probably just going to alienate teens that use it,"[22] he says.

Andrew Calderon began using hookahs when he was a teenager. Now twenty-three, the Astoria, New York, resident is old enough to legally smoke a hookah in a commercial establishment. He says, "Hookah allowed us to have a space for something to do—and unlike drinking or smoking [marijuana], we weren't going to get in trouble for it. It gave us a way to be part of the nightlife."[23]

For twenty-three-year-old Chatham, New Jersey, resident Asavari M., the appeal of using a hookah for her and for teenagers is that it is something that is usually done in groups. She says, "It's growing in popularity everywhere. It's more social for teens to sit in a group and smoke hookah than cigarettes. Hookah is more about the experience, whereas smoking cigarettes is more of a necessity."[24]

> "It's more social for teens to sit in a group and smoke hookah than cigarettes. Hookah is more about the experience, whereas smoking cigarettes is more of a necessity."[24]
>
> —Asavari M., resident of Chatham, New Jersey.

Conventional Cigarettes

Despite the growing popularity of e-cigarettes, flavored cigars, and hookahs, a significant population of young people continues to smoke conventional cigarettes. Sixteen-year-old Leah has been smoking paper-and-tobacco cigarettes for half her life. At eight or nine, when she began, she did not think about the possible impact on her health, and she had plenty of role models in her family who were smoking, too. "When I first started I figured, okay, one cigarette is not going to hurt me. And then, you know, one cigarette a day isn't going to hurt me," she says. "Two cigarettes a day isn't going to hurt me."[25]

At first Leah believed smoking was a choice she freely made, but she does not view her current habit as a choice. She admits to being addicted to smoking and knows it will be difficult to break her habit. She says, "That very first cigarette was my choice, and maybe even the second one. But now I've been smoking so long and I've smoked so much. I can try to quit, you know. That's a choice I can make. But you know, the wanting and the needing of the cigarette isn't a choice anymore."[26]

> "I play sports. And most of the people in my school who play sports do not smoke. They'll smoke over the summer. I have a lot of friends, and they'll say, 'Well, I'll smoke over the summer and then I'll quit for the school year so I can start my sports again.'"[27]
>
> —Ashley, student athlete.

Teens Smoke More in Summer

When it comes to susceptibility to the lures of smoking cigarettes, summertime seems to place teens at the greatest risk. Student athlete Ashley has seen this happen at her high school. She says, "I play sports. And most of the people in my school who play sports do not smoke. They'll smoke over the summer. I have a lot of friends, and they'll say, 'Well, I'll smoke over the summer and then I'll quit for the school year so I can start my sports again.'"[27]

According to Jon Macy, coordinator for the Monroe Tobacco Prevention and Cessation Coalition in Bloomington, Indiana, and an assistant professor in the department of applied health at Indiana University, several studies support Ashley's anecdotal evidence. He says more teens begin smoking in the months of June, July, and August than any other time of the year. Macy adds:

> The researchers felt that could be explained by the fact that teens have less adult-supervised time and spend more time outdoors during the summer. Also, a lot of tobacco companies' fiscal years end in June or July, when they might offer cigarettes at a discount to get rid of extra inventory. Young people are more price-sensitive than adults, because they typically have less disposable income to spend on cigarettes.[28]

A group of teens enjoys a seaside volleyball game. Studies have shown that more teens begin smoking during the summer months than at any other time of year.

Making Healthier Choices

Despite such newer pastimes as hookah usage, flavored small cigars and e-cigarette use by teenagers, efforts to get young people to enjoy smoke-free lifestyles have been paying off. Smoking rates for teenagers are currently at a forty-year low, according to the CDC. Eighteen years ago nearly 37 percent of teenagers were smokers. That number fell to about 16 percent by 2013. In comparison, about 18 percent of adults smoke today. "I think the bottom line is that our teens are choosing health,"[29] says Frieden.

It is also true that the number of teens who disapprove of smoking has been steadily increasing since 1996, according to the Monitoring the Future study, and the disapproval extends to dating. In 1996, for example, 71 percent of eighth grade students said they wanted to date nonsmokers. In 2004, 81 percent of students in the eighth grade expressed a preference for nonsmoking dating partners—a number that has not dipped in the ensuing ten years. The report found that teens who smoke would find their dating pool restricted.

Nevertheless, despite the reduction in overall tobacco use by young people, it is clear that new young smokers begin

Vape Named "Word of the Year"

The English language is not static; new words are added constantly in part as a result of America's changing culture. One of the entities that tracks the adoption of new words is the *Oxford Dictionaries*, which every year announces its word of the year. In 2013 that word was *selfie*, and the following year *Oxford Dictionaries* named *vape* as its most highly visible word. In selecting *vape*, the publication states: "Although there is a shortlist of strong contenders . . . it was vape that emerged victorious. You are thirty times more likely to come across the word vape than you were two years ago, and usage has more than doubled in the past year."

Quoted in Chris Perez, "Oxford English Dictionary Crowns 'Vape' Word of the Year," *New York Post*, November 18, 2014. http://blog.oxforddictionaries.com.

taking up the habit every day, replacing older smokers who succumb to tobacco-related deaths such as cancer, heart disease, and emphysema. Vince Willmore of the Washington, DC–based public advocacy group Campaign for Tobacco-Free Kids, says, "The fight against tobacco isn't over when we still have 2.7 million high school kids who smoke."[30] The statistic cited by Willmore suggests that antismoking advocates still have a lot of work to do, particularly as they face the new challenges of convincing young people that smoking e-cigarettes and small cigars and using hookahs are just as addictive and as dangerous as smoking conventional cigarettes.

Chapter Two

Why Do Teens Smoke?

The decision to smoke is not made in a vacuum. Teenagers are influenced by a variety of factors, including whether their parents or friends smoke; what they see on social media, in the movies, and on television; and while shopping in local stores.

Perhaps the biggest factor that influences their thinking about anything remotely dangerous is their developing brains. In fact, the same thinking that allows some teens to send nude selfies to their boyfriends or girlfriends without thinking through the possible consequences also comes into play in evaluating the risks associated with nicotine and tobacco. Cornell University neuroscientist B.J. Casey explains, "It isn't that teenagers can't make decisions. They are incredibly quick at doing that, but in an emotional setting, even when they know better, they often make the wrong ones."[31] The culprit is the teen brain.

Poor Impulse Control

Neuroscientists have learned that a person's brain does not reach full maturity before he or she has aged into the mid-twenties. Until that point the front part of the brain, or prefrontal cortex, where impulsiveness and emotion rule, is not yet well connected to the back part of the brain, where judgment occurs; hence, risks are more likely to be taken. Casey says,

> The teenage brain is stunningly different from that of an adult. While some areas—particularly those focused on motor control and hand/eye coordination—are as good as they will get, others, including the prefrontal cortex

just behind the forehead, which dictates complicated decision making and moderates social behavior, lag far behind. Nevertheless, adolescents are faced with decisions every day that can affect how or even whether they grow up.[32]

According to Frances Jensen, a neurologist and author of *The Teenage Brain*, the missing link between the front and back portions of the teenage brain is a fat called myelin. Myelin, which builds up slowly, facilitates connectivity between parts of the brain. So while the parts of the teenage brain "talk" to each other, they are not speaking fluently. Jensen says,

> Hence, teenagers are not as readily able to access their frontal lobe to say, 'Oh, I better not do this.' An adult is much more likely to control impulses or weigh out different factors in decisions, where a teenager may not actually have full online, in the moment capacity. And that's why we see this increase in risk—you know, classic sort of increased risky behavior.[33]

As the leading cause of preventable deaths in the country, smoking falls in the category of risky behaviors, especially given that the risks are well known. Moreover, brain anatomy at least partially accounts for why teenagers are so affected by what their friends do. Laurence Steinberg, author of *Age of Opportunity: Lessons from the New Science of Adolescence*, says, "Teenagers are motivated to take risks when the potential for pleasure is high, such as in unprotected sex, fast driving, or experimentation with drugs . . . especially when they are with friends."[34] Scientists now have visual proof that when teens do dangerous things in the presence of their friends, there is more activity in the pleasure centers of their brains than when they do dangerous things alone.

> "The teenage brain is stunningly different from that of an adult."[32]
>
> —B.J. Casey, Cornell University neuroscientist.

Bruce Simons-Morton of the National Institutes of Health (NIH) in Bethesda, Maryland, offers this supporting statistic: "Sixth, seventh and eighth graders were nine times more likely to smoke, and five times more likely to drink, if they had two or more friends who smoke and drank."[35]

Peer Pressure

When it comes to smoking, having friends who light up can put pressure on teens who do not join in, making them uncomfortable. Eleven-year-old Amber experienced this firsthand when she stood up to a friend who pressured her to smoke. "My best friend tried it, and she asked me to try. I said no. She got really mad at me. I felt bad, but I didn't want to hurt my life. There is way more stuff to do in the world than that,"[36] she says.

Sometimes friendships dissolve over the rift. "As the friends start smoking more and more, the nonsmoker has to make a decision: Either smoke or make new friends,"[37] says Connie Pechmann, a psychologist at the University of California at Irvine.

> "Sixth, seventh and eighth graders were nine times more likely to smoke, and five times more likely to drink if they had two or more friends who smoke and drank."[35]
>
> —Bruce Simons-Morton of the NIH.

In the end, though, friends have more impact on getting their peers to start smoking than to give up the habit, a Pennsylvania State University study concluded. Penn State professor Steve Haas, who worked on the study, says, "In order to become a smoker, kids need to know how to smoke, they need to know where to buy cigarettes and how to smoke without being caught, which are all things they can learn from their friends who smoke."[38] Unfortunately, peers have far fewer resources at their disposal to get their friends to effectively stop smoking.

Social Media

The influence of teen friendships extends into cyberspace, where teens sometimes brag about smoking on Facebook,

A teen checks his social media account. Many teens brag online about or post pictures of themselves smoking, which can influence others to smoke as well.

Tumblr, Instagram, and Vine. "Seeing GIFs on the Internet of cute guys smoking and puffing out that smoke makes it look like an art form,"[39] says fourteen-year-old nonsmoker Lily W. What teens see online can influence their offline behavior, too, researchers at the University of Southern California have found. In a study of more than fourteen hundred tenth graders in Los Angeles, researchers concluded that teens with few close friends who smoked or drank were more likely to be influenced to do so themselves after viewing photographs of other teens drinking or smoking.

According to the National Center on Addiction and Substance Abuse at Columbia University, 70 percent of twelve- to seventeen-year-olds spend at least some time on social media sites every day. And based on the center's 2011 back-to-school study of teenagers, it concluded that teens who enjoy social networking are five times more likely to use tobacco than teens who do not use social media. The reason cited was the abundance of images posted by teens who are boasting about smoking, making such behavior seem commonplace.

Parents Play a Role

Teens have another important relationship that is a good predictor of whether they will smoke: the relationship they have with their parents. Mothers and fathers can have a huge influence on whether their teens experiment with smoking or make the decision to avoid cigarettes. For instance, teens who frequently butt heads with parents who do not smoke or have forbidden their teens to smoke may have greater motivation to take up the habit. Danny McGoldrick, research director for the Campaign for Tobacco-Free Kids, says smoking enables teens to rebel against their parents at the same time they grow closer to their friends. Sixteen-year-old Tyler admits that part of his motivation for smoking is to rebel against his parents. He says, "I started smoking maybe about two years ago in my freshman year of high school, and I did it mainly because it was my choice. Some of my friends smoked and some of them didn't. I didn't do it to hang out with anyone, but I think maybe I did it to tick my parents off or my way of rebelling."[40] Heather had a similar motivation. "I did it because I was kind of a goody-goody and that was one way for me to rebel without having to cause my parents all kinds of heartache, although it's done that too,"[41] she says.

Although teenagers may be loath to admit it, what their parents say and do regarding smoking is just as influential as what their friends do. Parents who take a genuine interest in their teens' friends, schoolwork, and activities without overstepping their bounds can steer their children to healthier pursuits. Simons-Morton says, "Teens who reported that their parents were highly involved in their lives were about half as likely to smoke or drink than youth who felt their parents were not very involved."[42]

Children who grew up watching their parents smoke are not going to easily heed a parental message not to do as they are doing—although certainly some children may decide that

Can a TV Show Influence People to Smoke?

It may seem difficult to believe fictional characters could promote smoking. However, Thomas Frieden knows it is a fact. Before he worked for the CDC Frieden served as health commissioner for New York City; in that job he was responsible for launching initiatives to reduce smoking among city residents. His efforts largely paid off, with smoking rates falling by half in the general population. But for some reason smoking rates for white women did not fall. Perplexed, Frieden was determined to find out why.

He received the answer only after an anthropologist was retained to conduct focus groups—sessions with women who talked about their smoking habits—and a common factor emerged. The women all watched the same hugely popular television show, *Sex and the City*, featuring four glamorous single women. During most of the series Carrie, the lead character played by actress Sarah Jessica Parker, was often portrayed smoking cigarettes. The show has been credited with influencing women's attitudes about designer shoes and smoking. "It had a huge impact," Frieden says.

Quoted in Jennifer Dignan, "America's Bad Habit," *Scholastic Scope*, September 5, 2011, p. 19.

they do not want to repeat the missteps of their parents. But if cigarettes can easily be found around the home, teens are likely to be tempted to give them a try. Access to cigarettes in the house could mean not having to worry about skirting laws meant to prohibit young people from buying cigarettes.

Since teens cannot legally buy cigarettes, the ease with which they can acquire them is yet another important influence in whether they smoke. According to the Monitoring the Future study, the number of eighth and tenth graders who say they can easily find cigarettes has declined—with 39 percent of eighth grade students and 24 percent of tenth grade students admitting to finding it more difficult to acquire cigarettes.

Still, some 47 percent of eighth graders and 69 percent of tenth graders say acquiring cigarettes does not pose a problem.

Influence of Celebrities

Many teenagers love to follow the careers of celebrities, and the temptation to imitate them can be strong. So when celebrities like Johnny Depp, Paris Hilton, or Robert Pattinson are seen in photographs with vaping pens the subtle message is that e-cigarettes are cool. In fact, the sleek design of e-cigarettes may be giving a reboot to the tarnished image of smokers. Neal Benowitz of the University of California at San Francisco Center for Tobacco says, "People don't see as many people smoking anymore. All of a sudden, people are carrying around e-cigs so smoking behavior becomes renormalized."[43]

Of course, that is not to say that images of celebrities smoking paper cigarettes are difficult to find; they are not. Celebrities who have been photographed with cigarettes include singers Adele, Kelly Osbourne, Harry Styles, and Rihanna, and actresses Lana Del Rey, Whitney Port, Jessica Alba, Gwyneth Paltrow, and Kate Winslet. Moreover, some young people may be influenced to try cigars by celebrities such as Jay-Z, who is often photographed by the media smoking cigars and even has his own brand.

Robin Koval, chief executive officer of the American Legacy Foundation in Washington, DC, says that given their influence among young people, celebrities photographed with smoking materials might as well be considered spokespeople for tobacco companies. In 2014 her foundation created an antismoking commercial that aired during MTV's Video Music Awards. The commercial featured photographs of Orlando Bloom, Kristen Stewart, Robert Pattinson, Lady Gaga, Kirsten Dunst, and other celebrities, all with cigarettes and with the words "unpaid tobacco spokesperson" superimposed on them. Koval says,

We're fans, and we're trying to remind people that you can use all that influence you have for good and to think about it. . . . This is just another way to help bring aware-ness to the fact that we all have tremendous influence, we all have tremendous power now through social me-dia, paid media, all sorts of exposure. And we also have the opportunity to end this epidemic for good.[44]

According to experts, images of celebrities smoking, like this one of actor Robert Pattinson, strongly influence teenage fans to smoke in imitation.

Smoking in Movies

While some celebrities feel comfortable enough smoking to be photographed during their private moments, even more find themselves portraying characters who smoke on the big screen. There is evidence to suggest that teens who watch smoking on-screen are influenced to take up cigarettes themselves. Researchers at Dartmouth College's Norris Cotton Cancer Center in New Hampshire found that 44 percent of young people who try smoking do so as the result of viewing movies in which smoking is portrayed in a positive light.

Smoking Babies

The Southeast Asia nation of Indonesia has enacted no laws protecting minors from the health hazards of smoking. In Indonesia it is legal for children to buy cigarettes. Also, tobacco companies can advertise their products without restrictions. As a result of the country's lack of antismoking laws, an estimated 1 million smokers are under the age of sixteen.

One smoker was Aldi Rizal, who was already smoking forty cigarettes a day in 2010 when he was two years old. By 2015 a YouTube video depicting Aldi lighting one cigarette after another and puffing away had registered more than 27 million views. The boy, who lives in a hut with his family, gave up smoking at age five after public health officials stepped in because of the furor over the video.

Another two-year-old Indonesian smoker is Chairul. He is a two-pack-a-day smoker who sometimes smokes with his grandfather. His grandfather says Chairul is cranky when he does not smoke but does just fine when he smokes cigarettes and drinks coffee.

Matthew Myers, president of the Campaign for Tobacco-Free Kids, says, "Indonesia is the perfect example of what happens when you let the [tobacco] industry do whatever it wants to market to young people and the government does nothing to counteract it. It's a deadly combination."

Quoted in Jon Meyersohn and Dan Harris, "From Age 2 to 7: Why Are Children Smoking in Indonesia?," *20/20*, abcNEWS, September 9, 2011. http://abcnews.go.com.

Further, the study suggests that if motion picture executives removed all smoking scenes from movies rated PG-13, teen smoking rates could fall by as much as 20 percent. Study author James Sargent illustrates the difference between teens and adults: "Midway through their teens, they are by no means an adult like you and me. They're still somewhere between a two-year-old and a 25-year-old, and they're just more apt to be influenced. They have less control over that influence."[45]

One movie company whose products are produced exclusively for families and children, Walt Disney, adopted a smoking policy eight years ago. Under that policy movies containing smoking scenes receive an R rating (meaning anyone under seventeen must be accompanied by an adult to see the film). The studio will not seek an R rating only if the health consequences of smoking are apparent in the story or if the smoking is historically significant.

Sargent favors applying an R rating for all films that feature smoking. He says, "We're not saying you can't put smoking in the movie, and we're not saying that actors can't smoke while they're on screen. What we're saying is that if you do that, the movie should be rated R so it's harder for kids to watch."[46]

There is evidence indicating that teens whose parents let them watch R-rated films also have greater access to cigarettes than teens who are not permitted to watch those movies. That was one of the findings in a study on preventing smoking in youths conducted by medical student Angela C. Young and University of Massachusetts Medical School researchers Chyke Doubeni and Joseph DiFranza. They write: "This may be due to lax parental supervision associated with the ability to watch explicit movies. It also may be due to movie stars lighting up cigarettes and the tendency of teens to mimic the behavior of their idols."[47]

Confessions of a Hollywood Screenwriter

As a survivor of throat cancer, Hollywood screenwriter Joe Eszterhas has a unique perspective on smoking in movies. The one-time strident smoker used to believe everyone had a right to smoke and bristled over efforts to make the habit appear politically incorrect. His own cancer diagnosis altered his stance, as he explains in an essay he wrote for the *New York Times* eighteen months after his throat cancer was diagnosed in 1999. He writes: "I don't think smoking is every person's right anymore. I think smoking should be as illegal as heroin. . . . I want to do everything I can to undo the damage I have done with my own big-screen words and images."[48]

A talented screenwriter, Eszterhas appealed to other Hollywood writers to change the way in which smoking is depicted on film. He says:

> "A cigarette in the hands of a Hollywood star onscreen is a gun aimed at a 12- or 14-year-old."[49]
>
> —Joe Eszterhas, screenwriter.

A cigarette in the hands of a Hollywood star onscreen is a gun aimed at a 12- or 14-year-old (I was 12 when I started to smoke, a geeky immigrant kid who wanted so very much to be cool.) The gun will go off when that kid is an adult. We in Hollywood know the gun will go off, yet we hide behind a smoke screen of phrases like "creative freedom" and "artistic expression." Those lofty words are lies designed, at best, to obscure laziness. I know. I have told those lies. The truth is that there are 1,000 better and more original ways to reveal a character's personality [than through smoking].[49]

One in Three Movies Depicts Smoking

Many of Eszterhas's colleagues have yet to get the message. In 2010 about a third of movies considered appropriate for children featured characters who smoked, according to Jon Macy. But that situation may be changing. A study reported by *Chest*, a publication produced by the *Journal of the American College of Chest Physicians*, suggests that bigger studios no longer glorify smoking. However, this appears not to be true of small independent filmmakers. NPR news host Scott Simon says, "After surveying 447 popular movies from the past 15 years, *Chest* says that in most modern movies, cigarettes have become the new black hat, a prop to signal, da-da-da-dum, this is the bad guy. Now there is an important exception. The study says that independent films are much more likely to show sympathetic characters lighting up cigarettes."[50]

As an example, the *Chest* study cited the chain-smoking protagonists of the 1994 gangster comedy *Pulp Fiction*—bad guys, to be sure, but nevertheless characters the audience could find sympathetic. In fact, the movie's poster features the lead female character, portrayed by actress Uma Thurman, holding a cigarette between her fingers. *Pulp Fiction* was financed not by a major Hollywood studio but by Jersey Films, a small independent film production company.

The poster for the independent movie Pulp Fiction *shows actress Uma Thurman holding a lit cigarette. One study suggests that although bigger film studios no longer glorify smoking, smaller independent studios have not followed suit.*

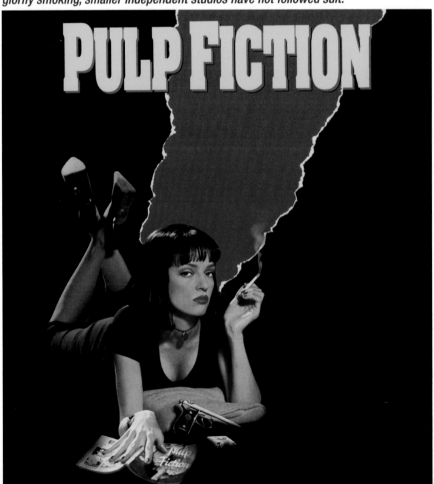

Holding Hollywood Accountable

One organization that is policing the movie industry is Scene Smoking, whose volunteer movie watchers scan new movies to determine whether they feature smoking in any form. The movies are then rated on its website, with smoke-free movies earning the pink lung symbol representing healthy lungs, and movies with many scenes featuring smoking characters meriting the black lung symbol. Recent movies that earned black lungs include the final installment in the Hobbit series, *The Hobbit: The Battle of Five Armies*, and *Boyhood*.

Also receiving a black lung was the 2010 film *The Tourist*, starring Johnny Depp, which earned its rating due to at least thirty incidents of smoking among six actors, including leading man Depp. *The Tourist* was the first major film to feature an actor smoking an e-cig on screen (and also speaking lines extolling its virtues to costar Angelina Jolie.)

In 2014 Boris Lushniak, acting US surgeon general, said he would like to see Hollywood producers portray smoking as much less glamorous. He said, "Anything that can be done to help reduce that imagery, to reduce that sense that smoking is a norm, is helpful. We would like to partner with the film industry to realize this has an effect on the health of our nation."[51]

E-Cig Commercials

While television ads for tobacco products have been banned since the early 1970s there are currently no such rules restricting TV advertisements for electronic cigarettes. In the absence of such regulation teens, along with adults, were exposed to commercials touting the virtues of e-cigs while watching network television shows that were popular with teens, including *The Bachelor*, *Big Brother*, and *Survivor*. According to a study by the medical journal *Pediatrics*, in general the number of electronic cigarette TV commercials viewed by twelve- to seventeen-year-olds grew 256 percent from 2011 to 2013. One such commercial features actress Jenny McCarthy in a slinky dress talking about how much she loves her Blu e-cig because it gives her the freedom to smoke anywhere and not have to worry about scaring away attractive men.

Some people are concerned that commercials such as the one in which McCarthy is featured will make e-cigs seem sophisticated and desirable to teenagers who are exposed to them. Jennifer Duke, who led the study quoted in *Pediatrics*, says,

> The tobacco industry and e-cigarette industry say that they are not advertising products to youth, but they are advertising products on a medium which is the broadest based medium in the country. . . . As e-cigarette advertisements increase for adults they are by default also increasing exposure to youth. It's hard to argue that only adults are seeing these ads.[52]

Duke is also concerned because to date there have not been any public service announcements produced by antismoking groups rebutting the claims of e-cig manufacturers. And Matthew Myers, president of the Campaign for Tobacco-Free Kids, wonders if tobacco companies are up to their same old tricks, this time with a new product. He says, "It's particularly disturbing precisely because Congress removed cigarette advertising from television because of the unique impact TV advertising has on young people. When e-cigarette manufacturers say they don't market to minors, it's déjà vu all over again."[53]

That teens see any commercials relating to smoking at all is significant given the findings of an older study published in 1997, examining twenty years of cigarette advertisements. Study author Richard Pollay, who was then affiliated with the

> "The tobacco industry and e-cigarette industry say that they are not advertising products to youth, but they are advertising products on a medium which is the broadest based medium in the country."[52]
>
> —Jennifer Duke, leader of medical journal Pediatrics study.

University of British Columbia in Vancouver, Canada, found that teenagers responded to cigarette advertisements three times as well as adults.

Reaching a Decision

As teenagers decide whether they will smoke, they are buffeted by many influences: friends, parents, movies, commercials, and what they read and see on social media. As they find themselves trying to make sense of a sometimes confusing set of impulses, benefits, and risks, they must do so with a brain that is geared more toward immediate gain in the now than to dangers that lurk in the future.

Chapter Three

What Price Do Teens Pay for Smoking?

About four thousand US teenagers light up their first cigarette each day. Approximately one-quarter of those will make it a daily habit. What may start out as an impulse or experiment can quickly go beyond their control because nicotine—the addictive ingredient in tobacco—is thought to be every bit as addictive as cocaine and heroin. In fact, addiction can literally begin with the first cigarette. "We have long assumed that kids got addicted because there were smoking 5 or 10 cigarettes a day. Now we know that they risk addiction after trying a cigarette just once,"[54] says Joseph DiFranza of the University of Massachusetts Medical School in Worcester, Massachusetts.

Such was the case for one teenage patient of physician Chyke Doubeni, who told him, "I remember it like yesterday. I saw my mother's cigarette on the dresser, picked it up, took one puff and I was hooked. I have tried many times to quit."[55] Of course, trying one or two cigarettes does not mean that a teen will end up a habitual smoker. According to DiFranza, about 25 percent of teens who experiment will end up hooked, with those who experience a near-instant form of relaxation from those early cigarettes at the greatest risk.

Preventable Deaths

Many teenagers who take their first puffs know they are doing something dangerous. Most young people can recite some of the ill effects that smoking can bring: lung cancer, emphysema, chronic obstructive pulmonary disease, and premature death. In fact, cigarette smoking accounts for more preventable deaths in America than any other activity. But knowing the possible consequences is not the turnoff one might expect. Dan Romer, research director of the Institute for Adolescent Risk Communication at the University of Pennsylvania's Annenberg Public Policy Center, says, "The idea of risk plays almost no role in their decision."[56] His studies lead him to believe that teens downplay their risks because they figure they will quit before much damage has been done. But that is not what usually happens.

And the health problems associated with smoking seem to be getting worse. "As inconceivable as it is, tobacco is even worse than we knew," says Thomas Frieden. "It appears cigarettes are getting more lethal. If you look at smokers over the years, even though they're smoking less, they're dying more."[57]

> "It appears cigarettes are getting more lethal. If you look at smokers over the years, even though they're smoking less, they're dying more."[57]
>
> —Thomas Frieden, director, US Centers for Disease Control and Prevention.

Teens who smoke cigars face the same risks as teens who smoke traditional cigarettes—with one exception: Cigars do not even have to be lit to affect health. "Merely holding an unlit cigar in the mouth exposes the user to tobacco and its poisons. This is due to the alkaline nature of the tobacco, as compared with the acidic tobacco of cigarettes, which makes it possible for nicotine to be absorbed even from an unlit cigar,"[58] according to the WHO.

What most teens do not realize is that smoking has immediate effects on their bodies, including their still developing brains. A 2014 report by the US surgeon general states, "The evidence is suggestive that nicotine exposure during adolescence, a critical window for brain development, may have lasting adverse consequences for brain development."[59] Teen smokers are more prone to mental illnesses, lower standardized test scores, and depression, the report says.

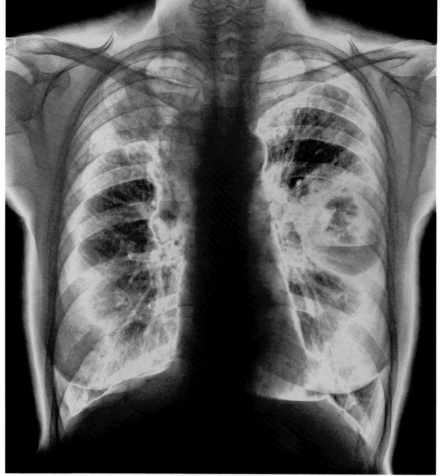

The red and yellow area in this enhanced X-ray shows a tumor caused by lung cancer, a condition that often results from smoking.

Addiction Is Quick

Nicotine, a chemical found in the tobacco plant, is a stimulant that reaches a smoker's brain within seconds of inhalation. The immediate result is that a smoker experiences a sense of well-being because the drug increases the amount of dopamine—the feel-good chemical in the brain. But that level quickly fades, requiring additional cigarettes to be smoked in order to get that feeling back. Within a relatively short time, young smokers might notice their growing dependence on cigarettes and the irritability, cravings, and sluggishness they experience when they do not light up.

Teenage brains are even more efficient at becoming addicted than adult brains. Frances Jensen explains that repeated exposure to nicotine enhances the synapses in the reward-seeking part of the brain. (Synapses are tiny components of the brain in which cells travel.) Says Jensen,

> They build a reward circuit around that substance to a much stronger, harder, longer, stronger addiction. . . . That is an important fact for an adolescent to know about themselves—they can get addicted faster. It also explains why and it also is a way to debunk a myth, by the way, that, oh, teens are resilient. They'll be fine, you know? He can adjust, go off and drink or do this or that. They'll bounce back. Actually, it's quite the contrary. The effects of substances are more permanent on the teen brain. They have more deleterious effects and can be more toxic to the teen than in the adult.[60]

Nicotine affects the body in other ways, too. Since these problems often do not materialize until a smoker is older, teens generally do not think about this when they start smoking. According to Robert Millman, addiction expert at New York–Presbyterian Hospital and Weill Cornell Medical Center, "It raises the heart rate, increases blood pressure, increases cardiac output and constricts blood vessels. All those things lead to long-term hypertension [high blood pressure] and heart diseases like congestive heart failure."[61]

> "The effects of substances are more permanent on the teen brain. They have more deleterious effects and can be more toxic to the teen than in the adult."[60]
>
> —Frances Jensen, neurologist.

Issues Girls Face

Girls develop addictions to nicotine more quickly than boys do, according to Marta De Borba-Silva. In addition, girls who smoke face health problems not experienced by boys. One of these health issues is an increased likelihood of developing osteoporosis, a thinning of the bones. Osteoporosis, which can lead to

Jury Says Teen Was Targeted by Tobacco Companies

At least eight thousand lawsuits have been filed against tobacco companies by smokers in Florida. One of those suits was filed by the family of Laura Grossman, who was fifteen when she began smoking cigarettes. The Broward County, Florida, woman remained a smoker for more than twenty years until she died from lung cancer in 1995. She was then thirty-eight and the mother of two children.

After her death her husband and children sued tobacco company R.J. Reynolds. In 2013 the family's attorney, Scott Schlesinger, alleged that the tobacco company's business model was built on attracting teenage smokers like Grossman. He suggested that when she was a teenager Grossman was too young to understand the risks she was taking even though they were spelled out on the warning labels of the cigarettes she smoked. Attorneys for R.J. Reynolds countered that Grossman had been adequately warned and was responsible for her own death. The jury found for the Grossmans, awarding them $37.5 million in damages.

bone breaks and a hunched-over appearance, usually does not develop until women go through menopause in their fifties.

Although the teenage years are normally a time for building bone mass, teenage female smokers lag in this area. Researchers at Children's Hospital Medical Center in Cincinnati, Ohio, discovered this when they spent three years following 262 girls between the ages of eleven and seventeen. As part of the study the researchers asked about the girls' habits and conducted bone density tests. The tests for nonsmokers showed a steady accumulation of bone growth during the three-year period; the smokers did not show any bone growth.

In addition to being more likely to fracture hips and other bones as they get older, female smokers who become pregnant—and their babies—are likely to suffer more complications. That is what happened to Amanda when she found herself with an unplanned pregnancy shortly after high school. The Wisconsin resident had been smoking for nearly a decade when she learned she was carrying a child. She continued to smoke during her pregnancy although she was aware of the risks. She had a hard time giving up cigarettes during past attempts to quit. Possible complications of smoking during pregnancy are miscarriages, underweight babies, and babies with allergies and breathing problems.

Amanda's baby was born two months early and weighed just three pounds. Most full-term babies weigh closer to seven or eight pounds and go home with their mothers in a day or two. Amanda's newborn was hospitalized for several weeks. When she finally came home the baby was often sick and had trouble gaining weight. When the baby developed allergies and asthma Amanda felt responsible, knowing that maternal smoking was the cause of her daughter's significant health problems.

A nurse cares for a hospitalized infant. Babies born to mothers who smoke can experience an array of health issues, including low birth weight and respiratory problems.

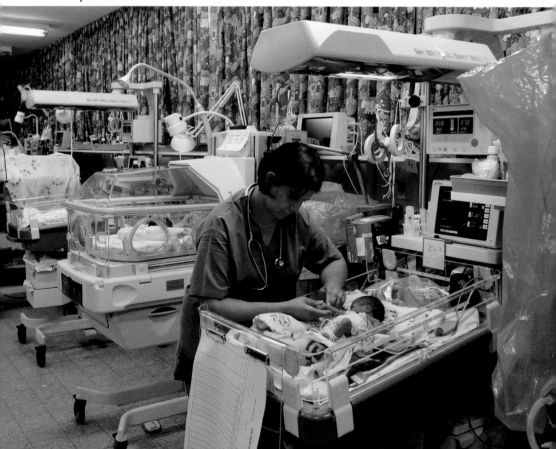

Chemicals in Cigarette Smoke

Even if she had not been pregnant Amanda should have been concerned about the four thousand chemicals found in burning cigarettes, chemicals with ominous-sounding names. For example, they include arsenic, a poison; benzene, a solvent derived from crude oil; cadmium, a metal found in batteries; hydrogen cyanide, a potent pesticide; and carbon monoxide, a killer when inhaled in large quantities.

Cigarettes also give off tar, which can cause lung cancer. According to the American Lung Association, lung cancer claims more lives than any other type of cancer, with nearly 160,000 Americans expected to die from the disease in 2015. In addition, the organization reports that each year some 220,000 Americans are diagnosed with lung cancer. Ninety percent of people who receive a lung cancer diagnosis are smokers, and the five-year survival rate for the disease is less than 18 percent. In addition to developing tumors, lung cancer sufferers may also contend with shortness of breath, chest pain, frequent infections, and fevers.

Premature Aging

What may be most shocking of all to teens is the idea that smoking will make them feel and look older than nonsmokers. Some of these signs of aging will be external, while others will not be visible to the naked eye. Young smokers are likely to remain unaware of the changes that are occurring in their lungs, which normally would still be expanding their capacity to take in air. In teen smokers, however, lung function begins to decline. For instance, a study focusing on seven hundred teens in the Boston area who began smoking at age fifteen found many to be exhaling 8 percent less air than a comparison group of nonsmokers. In fact, teen smokers' lungs stopped increasing their capacity to take in air a year before those of nonsmokers. Teens who continue to smoke into adulthood will often find themselves short of breath. For example, they might be unable to exercise as vigorously as nonsmokers. *Washington Post* reporter David Brown writes, "Lung function usually doesn't begin to decline until after age 45 in men. In those who started smoking as teenagers and kept at it, that change began almost 15 years earlier."[62]

A lung condition affecting smokers is bronchitis, an inflammation of the bronchial tubes—the main airways into the lungs. Bronchitis causes coughing and difficulty breathing. Another common lung ailment among smokers is emphysema, a disease in which the air sacs contained in the lung become damaged and less able to remove trapped air. Emphysema can cause coughing, difficulty breathing, lethargy, and lead to a weakened heart.

How smoking affects the heart and blood vessels can be seen at autopsy—the physical examination of the cause of death in a deceased person. According to CDC researchers, autopsies of smokers ages twenty-five to thirty-four killed by homicide or accidents were 50 percent more likely to show significant damage to the largest artery in the abdomen than in the autopsies of those who did not smoke. Similarly, the dead smokers' bodies revealed damage to blood vessels that, given time, could have eventually led them to suffer heart attacks.

Damage that shows up externally is harder to dismiss. For example, yellowed teeth, tooth loss, discolored fingernails and brittle hair can also make young people less attractive than their nonsmoking peers. So too can the appearance of wrinkles decades ahead of schedule. "People as young as 20 years old, they start to see fine lines, pigmentation, coarseness of the skin, and wrinkles around the mouth,"[63] says Joshua Zeichner, director of cosmetic and clinical research at Mount Sinai Hospital in New York City.

E-Cigs and Health

Although many people think e-cigarettes are safer than paper cigarettes, they too can affect the health of the users. A 2014 study published in the medical journal *Circulation* found that the vapors emitted by e-cigarettes contain many toxic chemicals and can lead to asthma, stroke, heart disease, cancer, and diabetes. The study found that chemical content varies among the various e-cigarette brands. However, in the e-cigarette brands analyzed in the *Circulation* study, the vapors included the chemicals formaldehyde and acetaldehyde. Formaldehyde is mostly used in the building industry as an ingredient for wood adhesives, while acetaldehyde is employed in the manufacture of perfumes and dyes and is also used as an additive in rubber manufacturing. Both chemicals are suspected carcinogens, which means they are believed to cause cancer. Says Laura Crotty Alexander, a professor of medicine at the University of

How Fast Do Smokers' Lungs Become Damaged?

Ryan Au, a teacher at a secondary school in Hong Kong, filmed a demonstration for his students to illustrate the damage that occurs to lungs after being exposed to as little as sixty cigarettes. Au, who noticed that a lot of students at his school were smoking, used two healthy sets of pig lungs for his demonstration.

He exposed both sets of pig lungs to air, showing what inflated lungs usually look like. Then he exposed one set of lungs to the smoke from sixty cigarettes. Teens who watched the video did not need a microscope to see the damage done to the lungs that were exposed to the cigarette smoke. The lungs that were exposed to smoke developed a yellow tinge, while the control group lungs—those that had not been exposed to smoke—remained a healthy pink. Then Au cut open the windpipe that fed both sets of lungs. The windpipe from the lungs exposed to smoke had turned black on the inside.

California at San Diego, "We started these studies so that we could advise our smoking patients on whether they should try switching to e-cigarettes. My data now indicate [e-cigarettes] might be the lesser of the two evils. But e-cigarettes are definitely not benign."[64]

Some countries have recognized the dangers of e-cigarettes and have taken action. While e-cigarettes have gained popularity in America, they have been banned in Canada, Singapore, Uruguay, Hong Kong, Brazil, Australia, and Lebanon.

Most experts agree that this newest form of smoking needs more study in order to be certain of its effects over time. One expert who believes that the newer e-cigarette products are less toxic than their predecessors is Neal Benowitz. He says, "I have to say that more recent products are much cleaner so analyses of products nowadays show much lower level of contaminants. They still have some toxins and there are still some concerns, but most likely, e-cigarette users are right that e-cig use, if they stop smoking, will be much less harmful."[65]

Some studies suggest that vaping might pose less of a long-term health hazard than smoking paper cigarettes. According to research presented at the 2012 gathering of the European Society of Cardiologists, there is evidence that vaping does not raise blood pressure and heart rates, factors that over time can lead to heart disease. Heart disease accounts for 40 percent of smoking-related deaths. The study was small with only forty-two smokers, half of whom were asked to smoke regular cigarettes and the other half to smoke e-cigarettes. After inhaling their respective cigarettes both groups underwent cardiac ultrasounds, an imaging process that allowed doctors to observe the subjects' hearts. Participants also had their blood pressures and pulses taken. Researchers concluded

> "People as young as 20 years old, they start to see fine lines, pigmentation, coarseness of the skin, and wrinkles around the mouth."[63]
>
> —Joshua Zeichner, director, Cosmetic and Clinical Research in Dermatology, Mount Sinai Hospital.

that the people who smoked paper cigarettes showed significant changes in cardiac function, while the vapers' tests were unchanged.

Should Youths Use Them?

However, like the regular cigarettes they are meant to replace, e-cigarettes contain addictive nicotine, and there is evidence that inhaling their vapors can harm bronchial cells in the lungs. "We know e-cigarettes are not safe for our youth," says Tim McAfee, director of the CDC's Office on Smoking and Health.

> While ENDS [electronic nicotine delivery system] may have the potential to benefit established adult smokers if used as a complete substitute for all smoked tobacco products, ENDS should not be used by youth and other adult non-tobacco users because of the harmful effects of nicotine and other risk exposures, as well as the risk for progression to other forms of tobacco use.[66]

In 2015 the California Department of Public Health produced a report on e-cigarette use in the state, noting that vapor produced by e-cigarettes contains at least ten chemicals known to cause cancer and birth defects. These vapors can also be inhaled by others who are near the person vaping. In addition, the liquid nicotine from the vape pen is poisonous if it is swallowed by a young child. So far, at least 154 poisonings of young children have occurred, one of them fatal. Ron Chapman, former director of the California Department of Public Health, has no doubt that e-cigarettes are harmful. He says, "I'm advising Californians, including those who use tobacco, to avoid using e-cigarettes. E-cigarettes . . . re-normalize smoking behavior and introduce a new generation to nicotine addiction."[67]

Some teens are listening to warnings issued by people like Chapman. Thirteen-year-old Brooke L. does not have Chapman's education or worldly experience, but she agrees with him. She says, "You may say, 'It's not a bad thing, I'm just smoking a pen—it's harmless.' But think about it: Smoking was in that sentence. And smoking is unhealthy. Period."[68]

Secondhand Smoke

Adverse effects of tobacco are not limited to the smokers of paper cigarettes and cigars; there is also a price to be paid for people who inhale the smoke of friends and family members who are smokers. Michael Weitzman, a researcher at New York University School of Medicine who studies the effects of secondhand smoke, says, "Almost one out of five people in the United States who die of lung cancer never smoked a cigarette in their life—but grew up around smokers."[69] Being around secondhand smoke can cause healthy nonsmokers to cough and

Breathing in the exhaled tobacco smoke of others, known as secondhand smoke, can result in health problems even for nonsmokers. These include hearing loss and lung cancer.

have irritated eyes and throats, but the situation is especially dangerous for people who suffer from asthma, a lung disorder in which inflamed airways make breathing difficult. Asthma can be managed with medication and by avoiding known triggers, but attacks are scary and can be fatal.

Jamason, eighteen, has suffered from asthma since he was a baby. Two years ago he had a severe asthma attack while working at a fast food restaurant. It was caused by coworkers who were smoking. Jamason began to wheeze and could not draw enough air into his lungs. He fought panic. Fortunately he was able to call his mother, who took Jamason to the hospital. He was admitted and spent four days receiving breathing treatments before he was discharged. Jamason is now understandably afraid to be around people who are smoking.

Smoking Leads to Hearing Loss

One unexpected consequence of breathing in the exhaled smoke of others is irreversible hearing loss. In a study of twelve- to nineteen-year-olds, Weitzman looked for an association between a byproduct of nicotine inhalation—a substance called cotinine—and hearing loss. He found it: Teens with the highest cotinine levels in their blood were 2.72 times more likely to suffer hearing loss than teens with no cotinine present. Most of the teens found to have hearing loss were unaware that they had the problem. Weitzman says, "I think that adolescents should know that smoking and being around friends who smoke may have lifetime consequences on their hearing."[70]

Researchers found a similar link between adults exposed to secondhand smoke and hearing loss. In a three-year study at the University of Manchester in Great Britain, more than 160,000 British adults ages forty to sixty-nine were given a hearing test; passive smokers were 28 percent more likely to have hearing loss than people who did not spend time around smokers.

Banning Smoking in Private Cars

According to the CDC, any exposure to secondhand smoke carries risk and therefore should be avoided. For teens riding in cars with adults or older teens who are smoking, that may mean summoning the courage to ask them to put out their cigarettes until the drive is over. While making such a request may be uncomfortable for the teen, it is preferable to putting up with the effects of secondhand smoke, which do not go away even if the car windows are down. The CDC estimates that one out of five middle school and high school students is exposed to secondhand smoke by riding in automobiles in which smoke is present. Because the interiors of automobiles are relatively small, exposure to secondhand smoke in a vehicle is thought to be worse than hanging out in a smoky bar. "The car is the only source of exposure for some of these children, so if you can reduce that exposure, it's definitely advantageous for health,"[71] says Brian King.

Some states have laws that protect minors from secondhand smoke in cars. They include Arkansas, California, Illinois, Louisiana, Maine, Oregon, and Utah. Michigan is not yet among those states, although some fourteen-year-old middle school students in Dundee, Monroe County, tried to bring about a statewide ban on the practice by forming their own organization, Smart Teens Opposed to Poisoning from Second-Hand Smoke. One of the teens, a girl named Lauren, says, "I'm sure everybody has been in a car where someone is smoking and didn't want to speak up. We want to change that. Think about all the kids that are exposed to second-hand smoke every day."[72]

A Public Health Issue

On the surface, deciding to smoke seems like a decision that affects only the smoker. In reality, with significant health hazards to nonsmokers who happen to be nearby, it is a public health issue with a staggering cost in medical bills, ill health, and shortened lives. As the European Society of Cardiologists points out, the number of deaths from smoking-related causes is expected to reach one billion in the twenty-first century, and many of those paying the ultimate price will have started as curiosity-seeking teenagers.

Chapter Four

Do Teens Respond to Antismoking Measures?

Fifty years have passed since the US surgeon general declared that smoking causes heart disease and lung cancer. During these years teen smoking rates have fallen, but 6 million teenagers have yet to get the message. To reach those teens—and the young people who will come after them—a variety of strategies is being employed. These include antismoking campaigns, which are increasingly being tailored to a younger demographic; school programs for elementary and middle school students; a mandate for the US Food and Drug Administration (FDA) to exercise control over cigarette marketing and manufacturing; and the efforts of individual states to pass laws limiting the exposure of teens to tobacco products while they are young enough to feel invincible.

One-time high school cheerleader Terrie Hall wished adults had tried harder to prevent her from smoking when she began at age seventeen. Her friends were smoking and so were her parents, and she thought having a cigarette was what adults did. Back then she had no idea what the next three decades of her life would have in store for her. If she had known she surely would have made different choices.

A two-pack-a-day smoker, Hall's first sign of trouble was a persistent sore throat that arrived in her mid-twenties. Fifteen years later Hall learned she needed radiation treatment for mouth cancer. As bad as that diagnosis was, it was not enough to make the North Carolina woman quit smoking. She reasoned that the radiation would kill the cancerous cells in her body.

But a few months later she had a new worry: The cancer had spread to her voice box—her larynx—and the larynx had to be removed. The operation left her unable to speak without the aid of a mechanical device inserted into her neck, giving her voice a robot-like quality. It was that inhuman sound that would make such a huge impact when Hall, in her early fifties, appeared in a two-minute public service announcement aimed at driving home to teenagers what could happen to them if they were to take that first puff.

Ugly Reality

As part of the CDC's Tips From Former Smokers campaign, Hall's 2012 antismoking spot attracted more viewers than any other spot in the series. YouTube alone has counted more than 4 million views of her starkly filmed spot in which she dresses for her day. In the hard-to-watch video, a nearly bald Hall matter-of-factly fits false teeth into her mouth, dons a blond wig, inserts into her neck the hands-free device that enables her to voice words, and with a touch of vanity conceals it with an attractive scarf.

Hall explained why she appeared in the public service announcement: "I hope it gets the message out to young people and middle-aged people that this can happen to you. I only smoked for 23 years and that's not that long to be diagnosed with any cancer. This is reality."[73] A short time later, cancer claimed Hall's life. She was fifty-three when she died.

Statistics suggest that Hall and other participants in the Tips From Former Smokers campaign may have accomplished their goal of scaring people into quitting. According to the CDC, one hundred thousand people who watched the public service spots were so horrified by seeing the unsparingly bleak images of real people ravaged by cancer that they quit smoking. That number was double what the CDC expected. Another 1.6 million smokers said they tried to quit because of the spots.

Teens Respond to Truth Campaign

How many teens gave up smoking or decided not to try it because of the CDC spots is unknown. However, there is substan-

Many programs and other resources are available to aid teens and adults alike who want to quit smoking.

tial data on an antismoking campaign, specifically designed for at-risk teens and preteens, that has been running for fifteen years. Truth is the brainchild of the Washington, DC–based nonprofit American Legacy Foundation, whose purpose is to prevent teenage smoking. Employing a mix of television, social media, and community events to get its message across, Truth has become a brand 80 percent of teens can identify. Other nonprofits recognize its success. "The Truth effort has been the envy of the entire public health community. [It is] very relevant, very contemporary,"[74] says American Cancer Society vice president Greg Donaldson.

Advertising professionals also praise the campaign. The trade journal *Advertising Age* ranked Truth among the top ad campaigns of the twenty-first century. Even more impressive is that in its first four years alone, the spots have convinced 450,000 teens not to smoke, according to the *American Journal of Public Health*.

Early ads zeroed in on ways tobacco companies mislead teens with their marketing messages. It was a message that spoke to young people used to tuning out messages about what is good for them. Ken August, an official in the tobacco control program for the California Department of Health, says, "You can't tell young people they're going to get sick, because they think they're invulnerable. But when you start telling them they're being used by adults—that really gets through."[75]

More recently, a 2015 Truth ad focuses on the lameness of teens who post smoking selfies on social media, declaring them to be less dateable because of their habit. Resembling a music video, the "Left Swipe Dat" commercial stars singers and Internet celebrities Becky G, Fifth Harmony, King Bach, Grace Helbig, Harley Morenstein, and Alpha. The latest entrant trying to reach the 6 million teenagers who still smoke is the FDA, which in 2009 was granted authority by Congress to regulate cigarettes. In that year the US Family Smoking Prevention and Tobacco Control Act, also known as the Tobacco Control Act, gave the government agency the authority to regulate the manufacturing, distribution, and marketing of tobacco products. Using that authority, in 2014 the FDA launched its own advertising campaign aimed at twelve- to seventeen-year-olds. The FDA is spending $600 million over a five-year period—paid for by tobacco companies under the Tobacco Control Act—on its Real Cost campaign that uses print, radio, television, and online outlets.

The Real Cost commercials illustrate sacrifices young people make when they smoke, whether they recognize those sacrifices or not. Teenagers are shown pulling off pieces of their flesh or yanking out their own teeth, then handing them over to cigarette vendors in exchange for packs of cigarettes. The message here is clear: There is a "real cost" associated with smok-

> "You can't tell young people they're going to get sick, because they think they're invulnerable. But when you start telling them they're being used by adults—that really gets through."[75]
>
> —Ken August, California Department of Health.

Buying Cigarettes Is Her Job

Connie Lau of Castro Valley, California, has an unusual job. Two years shy of being old enough to legally buy cigarettes, she purposely visits stores in hopes of being sold cigarettes by careless cashiers who do not bother to card her. As an undercover shopper for her local police department, Lau is doing her part to keep store operators from supplying her fellow teens with smokes and breaking the law.

Lau does not visit the stores alone. A police officer selects which retailers to visit and waits outside while she attempts to make the purchase. If she is carded, she admits she is sixteen and leaves the store without the cigarettes. That happens most of the time. However, when she is sold cigarettes without being carded, the police officer comes into the store and writes a ticket. In more than 150 store visits, Connie was sold cigarettes fifteen times. "The first time I was sold cigarettes was exciting. Afterward, when the officer was writing the ticket, the cashier kept saying, 'She looked old enough!' She stared at me the entire time. I smiled and waved," Lau says. Once businesspeople get caught in the sting, she maintains, they will be more careful in the future.

Quoted in *Scholastic Choices*, "Secret Agent Girl," April/May 2012, p. 21.

ing that goes beyond the money it takes to buy cigarettes—that cost is paid for in a lifetime of poor health.

Of course the FDA's expenditure is but a fraction of the $8 billion the tobacco industry spends on marketing its products, according to CDC statistics. The industry's deep pockets allow it to spend lavishly on in-store sales displays and to offer consumers deep discounts on cigarette cartons. Still, the Real Cost ads are tailored to specific groups of at-risk youths such as Hispanics, Asians, African Americans, and members of the LGBT community.

School Programs Can Make a Difference

While it is too soon to know the effectiveness of the Real Cost ads, efforts to convince young people to enjoy smoke-free lifestyles have been paying off—despite such newer pastimes as hookah usage, flavored small cigars, and e-cigarettes. Among the teens who have been influenced by antismoking messages is fifteen-year-old Kyle H., who says multiple influences helped dissuade him from trying tobacco. "It was a combination of early influence at home—my parents don't smoke—and health classes at school that backed it up," he says. "That influenced me more than anything else. I've been taught what smoking does to people. It's really disgusting, and I don't want that to happen to me."[76]

> "I've been taught what smoking does to people. It's really disgusting, and I don't want that to happen to me."[76]
>
> —Kyle H., fifteen years old.

Still, the record shows that school-based antismoking programs could stand improvement. "Standard school-based smoking-prevention programs are just not as successful as we would like,"[77] says Brian Primack, director of the Program for Research on Media and Health at the University of Pittsburgh School of Medicine in Pennsylvania. In studying the issue he found that nearly 25 percent of ninth graders who took a media literacy class, which helped them look more critically at messages they receive from popular culture, were less likely to smoke compared to 16 percent of ninth graders who took a standard antismoking program dealing with resisting peer pressure. "We need to see if this type of program sticks with people,"[78] Primack says.

To find out what programs are effective, an international organization of medical researchers reviewed more than one hundred studies on school-based antismoking programs. In doing so, the Cochrane Collaboration concluded that the most effective programs did more than educate students about the perils of smoking. They also taught students how to be better problem solvers and make better decisions.

The FDA's Role

In 2014 FDA officials said they planned to start exercising their right to regulate e-cigarettes, cigars, pipe tobacco, and hookahs to help keep them away from minors.

For example, under the proposed changes manufacturers would be asked to restrict sales to minors, who must show proof of age, and eliminate giving away free samples of their products, which helps to motivate more new people to try those products. In addition, manufacturers would be forced to reveal the ingredients in their products, post warning labels approved by the government agency, and stop making health claims that are unsupported by scientific studies.

Some doubt that these strategies will be enough to keep teens from adopting these newer tobacco products. For example, it would still be possible for minors to purchase e-cigarettes online and to indulge in the candy-flavored liquid nicotine teens are drawn to. Less than optimistic about the FDA's proposed

Varieties of candy-flavored nicotine like the ones pictured here are especially attractive to teens, who consume them using e-cigarettes.

What If Pharmacies Did Not Sell Cigarettes?

People go to drugstores to get prescriptions filled, visit walk-in health clinics, and purchase other products that can help them to lead healthier lifestyles. But the front of many of these stores contains a display of known killers: cartons of cigarettes available for purchase.

In 2014 the second largest pharmaceutical chain in America, CVS, became the first national chain to stop selling cigarettes and other tobacco products. These items are no longer sold at any of the chain's more than seventy-five hundred stores. The decision costs the company $2 billion in lost sales annually. Troy Brennan, CVS's chief medical officer, explains why the company made the decision. He says, "The question we get from health care providers is: how serious are you about health? This decision indicates exactly how serious we are."

Although CVS is the first giant retailer to refuse to sell cigarettes, other smaller pharmacies had already taken that step. Bans at these pioneering stores have already demonstrated that when smokers have a hard time buying cigarettes they will smoke less. In fact, Brennan estimates that sixty-five thousand lives could be saved every year if all American pharmacies ceased tobacco sales.

CVS's decision is opposed by Audrey Silk, a leader of the smokers' rights group Citizens Lobbying Against Smoker Harassment. She says, "They sell candy. They sell beer. . . . It's a perception war. . . . Tobacco is legal. They're engaging in public coercion by not selling cigarettes."

Quoted in Stephanie Kraus, "Ending Teen Smoking," *Time for Kids*, October 27, 2014.

Quoted in Jayna O'Donnell and Laura Ungar, "CVS Stops Selling Tobacco, Offers Quit-Smoking Programs," *USA Today*, September 3, 2014. www.usatoday.com.

changes is Michael Siegel, a professor at Boston University School of Public Health, who criticizes the Tobacco Control Act because of the loopholes it leaves in place. For example, the act would allow the FDA to require cigarette companies to reduce nicotine levels. Should that happen, Siegel says, smokers would compensate by smoking additional cigarettes and inhaling each of them more deeply. That in turn would cause them to introduce more cancer-causing tar into their lungs. Adds Siegel,

> The bill's basic problem is that it creates the appearance of regulation without allowing actual regulation. Take the issue of cigarette flavorings. Under the bill, most flavorings—including chocolate, cherry, strawberry, banana and pineapple—would be banned. But not menthol. Yet of all the cigarette flavorings, only menthol is being used by cigarette companies, and evidence suggests that it helps entice and addict young people, especially African Americans.[79]

State Actions

In the absence of FDA regulation, which by 2015 was still being studied, individual states have been enacting their own laws to protect the health of young people. Forty-two states, including Michigan, have banned e-cigarette sales to minors, and two states, Minnesota and North Carolina, are taxing them. New Jersey, North Dakota, and Utah have also banned the indoor use of e-cigarettes in restaurants, workplaces, and bars.

Some state lawmakers have proposed raising the legal smoking age to twenty-one, only to have those measures fail to win enough votes in their legislatures to pass. Those states include Utah, Colorado, New Jersey, Massachusetts, Maryland, and Hawaii. In Colorado, senators Steve King and Vicki Marble were on opposite sides of the issue. King argued that it made sense to make twenty-one the legal age to buy tobacco since it is also the legal age for gambling and drinking. Marble's counterargument seemed equally logical. "If we have our military age at 18, they should be able to smoke. They're old enough,"[80] she said.

At least one city government has taken action on its own. In November 2013 New York City became the first city to raise the legal purchase age of tobacco to twenty-one.

Taxes on Tobacco

Another way states try to limit teen access to cigarettes is through levying higher sales taxes on them. The price of cigarettes has been increasing dramatically over the past two decades, and, not surprisingly, substantial taxes added on to the price of cigarettes have a more profound impact on young smokers than they do on adult smokers with steady jobs.

To see the correlation, all one has to do is compare the smoking rates of high school teens in Kentucky, which has one of the lowest cigarette taxes in the country, with that of New York State, which has the highest. In 2013, 25 percent of high school students in Kentucky were smoking. In contrast, 8.5 percent of high school students in New York City were reported to be smoking. The state of New York levies a tax of $4.35 on a pack of cigarettes, and residents of New York City must pay an additional $1.50 in taxes per pack to buy their cigarettes. The total cost per pack to smokers in New York City is now about $13. At that price, cigarettes are a luxury item for many teens.

Tobacco companies also believe higher prices are bad for business. A once confidential memo produced by tobacco company Philip Morris gave voice to that concern. "Of all the concerns . . . taxation . . . alarms us the most. Price . . . is the main driving force for quitting,"[81] it reads.

An editorial in *USA Today* suggests that a way to lower the smoking rate of all Americans would be to compel low sales tax states like Kentucky to raise their rates. Says the newspaper:

> It's hard to think of a tax with more upside than one on cigarettes. Tobacco taxes improve public health, saving money. They raise money that can be used for quit lines [smoking cessation hotlines] and antismoking campaigns. And they deter young people from slowly killing themselves. If the nation is to continue its antismoking progress, it is time for the low-tax states to step up.[82]

Street Dealers

Sometimes, however, attempts to raise cigarette taxes fail. That was the case in Ohio, where the tax rate on cigarettes is below the national average and smoking rates have actually been going up. When Ohio governor John Kasich tried to raise the tax rate by just thirty cents a pack in 2015, to bring it in line with the national average, he was rebuffed by state legislators. He also lacked the support of antismoking groups who thought the raise was not enough to make a difference. Undeterred, Kasich has since decided to ask for a boost to a dollar a pack. At that level antismoking groups project the state might see sixty thousand fewer young people take up smoking and seventy thousand adults decide to give up their habits.

As one might expect, raising the price of cigarettes is not popular with smokers. Surely many smokers feel like Toni Leach, a resident of Coshocton, Ohio, who says, "When is the discrimination going to stop against smokers? They have already made it so we can't smoke inside places, made it so we can't smoke outside places and made it so we spend more money on cigarettes than we do on fuel. It's ridiculous!"[83]

Critics point out that raising taxes on cigarettes leads to the creation of a robust underground cigarette sales industry willing to sell inexpensive cigarettes to minors. Perhaps the best-known member of that illegal trade was Eric Garner, the New York City street seller who died after being placed in a choke hold by police while allegedly resisting arrest. Garner's death raised many important civil rights issues—African American activists and others believed Garner was the victim of police brutality and had been targeted for harsh treatment by white officers because he was black. Nevertheless, an aspect of the case that was given far less attention is the fact

"It's hard to think of a tax with more upside than one on cigarettes. Tobacco taxes improve public health, saving money. . . . And they deter young people from slowly killing themselves."[82]

—USA Today *editorial.*

Cartons of cigarettes available for purchase sit displayed on store shelves. Steep taxes on cigarettes make them more difficult for teens with limited income to buy than they are for higher-earning adults.

that he was placed under arrest for selling loose cigarettes—a crime in New York City and virtually everywhere else in America as well.

Customers who buy loose cigarettes evade the taxes assessed by the state and city, making the cigarettes cheaper. Also, sellers of loose cigarettes do not adhere to laws that make it illegal for stores to sell cigarettes to minors. Virtually anybody, no matter how young, can buy loose cigarettes on the street. Therefore, in addition to denying the state and city the tax revenue they are due (for New York that represents about $1.8 billion annually), the underground market provides an easier way for minors to acquire tobacco.

Teen Activists

As adults continue to mull over the best ways to discourage young people from smoking, some teens refuse to sit on the sidelines of the issue. These teens are having an impact that far outweighs their years. Among them are Calitta Jones, Brian Bell, Shanicee Dillon, and Jeremiah Carter, who convinced their hometown of St. Paul, Minnesota, to ban convenience stores from selling candy cigarettes and toy lighters. The quartet worked with St. Paul council member Melvin Carter (no relation to Jeremiah Carter) to build public opinion in favor of the ban after they visited neighborhood stores looking for tobacco advertising that could influence the behavior of children. Almost by accident, they discovered the inappropriate toys after Dillon's two-year-old sister spotted them and wanted to play with them. Councilman Carter says, "Kids have power when it comes to public policy . . . if they're willing to roll up their sleeves and get at it. Young people have the ability to look around their community, figure out the problems, and solve them."[84]

In 2014 dozens of Canadian students staged a protest at a movie theater in Toronto where the film *St. Vincent* was being shown. The students were upset that the film was not given an adult rating despite the fact that its lead character, portrayed by Bill Murray, smoked in many scenes. As passersby looked on they shouted, "Lights, camera, action, cut smoking off the screen for children and teens."[85]

> "Young people have the ability to look around their community, figure out the problems, and solve them."[84]
>
> —Melvin Carter, city council member, St. Paul, Minnesota.

Preventing Illness and Death

One of the demonstrators, Mousavi Nia, said films that depict smokers make them seem charismatic and sexy. "It makes it seem like smoking is the norm, that smoking is OK. That's why I think it's such a big problem."[86] The demonstrators hope ultimately to see all movies in which smoking is depicted earn ratings that would require anyone under eighteen to be accompanied by an adult in order to see them.

Sixteen-year-old Alexus Galindo is less concerned about smoking in movies than she is about smoking in parks in her hometown of Ector County, Texas. Ector County has a higher smoking rate than the state average. She has watched her grandparents become ill from smoking-related problems and sees students at her high school using e-cigarettes. Concern for their well-being prompted her to become a member of the X-Out Youth Leadership Coalition. As an ambassador for this organization that seeks to dissuade teens from alcohol and drug use, Alexus talks to students, encouraging them not to smoke. She would like to see a city ordinance banning e-cigarettes in some places.

Meanwhile, in the small town of Putnam, Connecticut, which covers barely three square miles (8 sq km), a high school senior spent two years trying to make the town fathers declare its parks smoke free. Michael LaRochelle met with state representatives, town selectmen, and the local department of health; the latter agreed to absorb the cost of creating signs announcing the policy. As a result of Michael's lobbying efforts, the town agreed to create a voluntary no-smoking policy in its parks. This stopped short of the ordinance Michael had in mind that would have levied fines if violated, but he still views it as a victory. He says, "A lot of teenagers don't think we can make a difference. Maybe now that they see I actually got this done they will try to do something on their own."[87]

Each effort that succeeds, from raising sales taxes to the creation of the latest antismoking advertisement designed specifically for teens, plays an important role in limiting the number of new young smokers. By convincing them to say no to smoking as teens they can be spared a lifetime of preventable illness and early deaths.

Introduction: A New Generation Decides About Smoking

1. Quoted in Fred Tasker, "Teens, Tobacco & Truth," *Miami Herald*, September 18, 1998, p. 1F.
2. Quoted in Polly Sparling, "A Do or Die Decision," *Current Health*, November 2008, p. 9.
3. Jerome Manansala, "Teen Doesn't Want to See Life Go Up in Smoke," *New Expression*, January/February 1994, p. 5.
4. Marta De Borba-Silva, "The Alarming Trend of Teen Girl Smoking," *Pediatrics for Parents*, August 2007. www.peds forparents.com.
5. De Borba-Silva, "The Alarming Trend of Teen Girl Smoking."
6. Quoted in Jillian Lloyd, "Views on Teen Smoking from Denver Schoolyard," *Christian Science Monitor*, September 22, 1997, p. 1.

Chapter One: Who Is Smoking What?

7. Quoted in Katie Abbondanza, "Clouds of Confusion," *Girls' Life*, October/November 2014, p. 72.
8. Quoted in Abbondanza, "Clouds of Confusion."
9. Quoted in Lloyd D. Johnson, Patrick M. O'Malley, Richard A. Milech, Jerald G. Bachman, and John E. Schulenberg, "Key Findings on Adolescent Drug Use Overview," *National Survey Results on Drug Use, 1975–2014*, Ann Arbor, MI: Monitoring the Future, 2015, p. 8. www.monitoringthe future.org.
10. Quoted in Alexandra Sifferlin, "Teen Smoking Is Way Down. But What About E-Cigs?," *Time*, June 12, 2014. http://time .com.
11. National Institute on Drug Abuse, "Drug Facts: Electronic Cigarettes," September 2014. www.drugabuse.gov.
12. Quoted in Stephanie Chuang, "Growing Use of Vaporizers Alarms Health Officials," *NBC Bay Area*, October 1, 2013. www.nbcbayarea.com.

13. Quoted in Deborah Netburn, "The E-Cigarette Boom: Study Finds 466 Online Brands, 7,700 Flavors," *Los Angeles Times*, June 17, 2014. http://touch.latimes.com.

14. Quoted in Karen Kaplan, "Move Over Tobacco: US Teens Now Prefer E-Cigarettes, Study Finds," *Los Angeles Times*, December 16, 2004. http://touch.latimes.com.

15. Quoted in Robin Lally, "Flavored Cigars Luring Teens and Young Adults," *Rutgers Today*, May, 14, 2014. http://news.rutgers.edu.

16. Quoted in Anna Edney, "Cherry Cigars Entice Teens with Candy Flavors, Researchers Say," *Businessweek*, May 8, 2014. www.businessweek.com.

17. Quoted in David Graham, "Smoke and Mirrors: Teens Are Falling for Mint-Chocolate Flavoured, Honey-Dipped, Sugar-Tipped Baby Cigars Because They're Sweet, They're Cheap and They're Easy to Get," *Toronto Star*, March 31, 2006, p. D1.

18. Quoted in Edney, "Cherry Cigars Entice Teens with Candy Flavors, Researchers Say."

19. Quoted in Johnson, O'Malley, Milech, Bachman, and Schulenberg, "Key Findings on Adolescent Drug Use Overview," p. 46.

20. Quoted in Michelle Healy, "High-Income Teens More Likely to Use Hookahs," *USA Today*, July 7, 2014.

21. Quoted in "Tobacco: Deadly in Any Form or Disguise," WHO Library Cataloguing-in-Publication Data, 2006, p. 24.

22. Quoted in Rachel Feltman, "1 in 5 Teens Smoke Hookah; Half Think It's Healthful," *Washington Post*, July 10, 2014.

23. Quoted in Chelsie Rose Marcus and Erin Durkin, "Hookah Smoking Is Common Among Teens, Especially the Wealthy," *New York Daily News*, July 6, 2014. www.nydailynews.com.

24. Quoted in Marcus and Durkin, "Hookah Smoking Is Common Among Teens."

25. Quoted in *FDA Consumer*, "On the Teen Scene: Young People Talk with FDA Commissioner About Smoking," January/February, 1998.

26. Quoted in *FDA Consumer*, "On the Teen Scene."
27. Quoted in *FDA Consumer*, "On the Teen Scene."
28. Quoted in Dann Denny, "Teens More Likely to Start Smoking During Summer, Study Says," *Herald-Times*, June 9, 2009.
29. Quoted in Sifferlin, "Teen Smoking Is Way Down. But What About E-Cigs?"
30. Quoted in Kim Painter, "Teen Smoking Hits Record Low," *USA Today*, June 13, 2014, p. 1A.

Chapter Two: Why Do Teens Smoke?

31. Quoted in Gloria Hochman, "When 'Life Is on Fire,'" *Philadelphia Inquirer*, February 1, 2015, p. G6.
32. Quoted in Hochman, "When 'Life Is on Fire.'"
33. Quoted in *Fresh Air*, "Why Teens Are Impulsive, Addiction-Prone and Should Protect Their Brains," NPR, January 28, 2015. www.npr.org.
34. Quoted in Hochman, "When 'Life Is on Fire.'"
35. Quoted in Jason Carroll and Christy Feig, "Ahead of the Curve," CNNfn, January 23, 2001. www.cnn.com.
36. Quoted in Sparling, "A Do or Die Decision," p. 9.
37. Quoted in Sparling, "A Do or Die Decision," p. 9.
38. Quoted in *Indian Express*, "Peer Pressure Is Weaker for Teens to Quit Smoking," Press Trust of India, June 13, 2014. http://indianexpress.com.
39. Quoted in Abbondanza, "Clouds of Confusion."
40. Quoted in *FDA Consumer*, "On the Teen Scene."
41. Quoted in *FDA Consumer*, "On the Teen Scene."
42. Quoted in Carroll and Feig, "Ahead of the Curve."
43. Quoted in Chuang, "Growing Use of Vaporizers Alarms Health Officials."
44. Quoted in Ariana Bacle, "What's with Those 'Unpaid Tobacco Spokesperson' Ads During the VMAs?," *Entertainment Weekly*, August 25, 2014. www.ew.com.
45. Quoted in Conan Milner, "Surgeon General Wants R Rating for Movie Smoking," *Epoch Times*, January 29, 2014. www.theepochtimes.com.

46. Quoted in Milner, "Surgeon General Wants R Rating for Movie Smoking."
47. Angela C. Young, Chyke Doubeni, and Joseph DiFranza, "Preventing Smoking in Youths," *Pediatrics for Parents*, p. 13.
48. Joe Eszterhas, "Hollywood's Responsibility for Smoking Deaths," *New York Times*, August 9, 2000. www.nytimes.com.
49. Eszterhas, "Hollywood's Responsibility for Smoking Deaths."
50. Scott Simon, "Smoking and the Movies," *Weekend Edition*, NPR, August 20, 2005. www.npr.org.
51. Quoted in Monte Morin, "Surgeon General to Hollywood: Kick the Cigarette Habit," *Los Angeles Times*, January 17, 2014. http://articles.latimes.com.
52. Quoted in Michelle Healy, "An 'Explosion' of Youth Exposure to E-Cigarette Ads," *USA Today*, June 2, 2014. www.usatoday.com.
53. Quoted in Healy, "An 'Explosion' of Youth Exposure to E-Cigarette Ads."

Chapter Three: What Price Do Teens Pay for Smoking?

54. Quoted in Jane E. Brody, "In Adolescents, Addiction to Tobacco Comes Easy," *New York Times*, February 12, 2008.
55. Quoted in Young, Doubeni, and DiFranza, "Preventing Smoking In Youths."
56. Quoted in Chris Woolston, "Teen Smokers," *HealthDay*, March 11, 2014. http://consumer.healthday.com.
57. Quoted in Morin, "Surgeon General to Hollywood: Kick the Cigarette Habit."
58. Quoted in WHO Library Cataloguing-in-Publication Data, "Tobacco: Deadly in Any Form or Disguise," 2006, p. 23.
59. US Department of Health and Human Services, *The Health Consequences of Smoking—50 Years of Progress: A Report of the Surgeon General, 2014*. Washington, DC: US Department of Health and Human Services, 2014. www.surgeongeneral.gov.

60. Quoted in *Fresh Air*, "Why Teens Are Impulsive, Addiction-Prone and Should Protect Their Brains."

61. Quoted in C. Claiborne Ray, "The Nicotine Blast," *New York Times*, September 16, 2008. http://query.nytimes.com.

62. David Brown, "Report: Teen Smoking Hastens Heart, Lung Decline," *Washington Post*, March 8, 2012.

63. Quoted in Linzie Janis, "No Smoking," *World News with Diane Sawyer*, February 4, 2014.

64. Quoted in Janet Raloff, "Health Risks of E-Cigarettes Emerge," *Science News*, June 3, 2014. www.sciencenews .org.

65. Quoted in Chuang, "Growing Use of Vaporizers Alarms Health Officials."

66. Quoted in CDC, press release, "More than 16 Million Children Live in States Where They Can Buy E-Cigs Legally." www.cdc.gov.

67. Quoted in Eryn Brown, "California Announces Campaign to Combat Use of E-Cigarettes," *Los Angeles Times*, January 28, 2014. http://touch.latimes.com.

68. Quoted in Abbondanza, "Clouds of Confusion."

69. Quoted in Karina Hamalainen, "Substance Abuse: Say What?," *Scholastic Choices*, November/December 2011, p. 7.

70. Quoted in Hamalainen, "Substance Abuse: Say What?"

71. Quoted in Lindsey Tanner, "Smoking in Cars a Threat to Teens," *Guelph Mercury*, February 7, 2012, p. B2.

72. Quoted in Caitlin VanOverberghe, "Dundee Students Want to Ban Smoking in Cars with Minors," *Monroe* (MI) *News*, April 9, 2014. www.monroenews.com.

Chapter Four: Do Teens Respond to Antismoking Measures?

73. Quoted in Jessica Ravitz and Saundra Young, "Antismoking Symbol Reveals 'Worst Moment,'" CNN, March 16, 2012. www.cnn.com.

74. Quoted in Beth Herskovits, "Companies: Corporate Profile— Legacy's Truth Finds Receptive Audience," *PR Week*, June 12, 2006, p. 9.

75. Quoted in Woolston, "Teen Smokers."
76. Quoted in Sparling, "A Do or Die Decision."
77. Quoted in Andrew M. Seaman, "Media Literacy Promising for Teen Antismoking Education," Reuters, January 14, 2014. www.reuters.com.
78. Quoted in Seaman, "Media Literacy Promising for Teen Antismoking Education."
79. Quoted in *Los Angeles Times*, "Tobacco Regulations Are No Regulations At All," June 3, 2009. http://articles.la times.com.
80. Quoted in Kristen Wyatt, "Colorado Lawmakers Want to Ban All Teen Smoking," *Daily Sentinel*, February 1, 2014. www.gjsentinel.com.
81. Quoted in Editorial Board, "States with the Highest Excise Taxes Have Some of the Lowest Teen Smoking Rates," *USA Today*, March 28, 2013. www.usatoday.com.
82. Quoted in Editorial Board, "States with the Highest Excise Taxes Have Some of the Lowest Teen Smoking Rates."
83. Quoted in Jessica Balmert, "Ohio Smokers Targeted by Proposed Tax Hike," (Freemont, OH) *News Messenger*, February 17, 2015. www.thenews-messenger.com.
84. Quoted in Dan Risch, "Kids Take On the Tobacco Companies," *Current Health Kids*, October 2011, p. 9.
85. Quoted in Jane Gerster, "Group Says Youth Should Not See Films That Depict Smoking," *Toronto Star*, September 7, 2014.
86. Quoted in Gerster, "Group Says Youth Should Not See Films That Depict Smoking."
87. Quoted in Francesca Kefalas, "Putnam Teen on Quest to Ban Smoking in Local Parks," *AP Regional State Report*, October 26, 2013.

American Cancer Society

250 Williams St. NW
Atlanta, GA 30303
phone: (800) 227-2345
website: www.cancer.org

The American Cancer Society is a nationwide, community-based volunteer organization dedicated to preventing cancer and funding research for cures. Visitors to the website can view infographics on the true cost of smoking and learn the latest cancer facts and statistics.

American Legacy Foundation

1724 Massachusetts Ave. NW
Washington, DC 20036
website: www.legacyforhealth.org

The largest nonprofit public health organization in America dedicated to wiping out teenage smoking, American Legacy is also the sponsor of the well-respected Truth campaign. Visitors to the website can watch videos on hookah safety, smoking in the movies, and youth activism.

American Lung Association

5 W. Wacker Dr., Suite 1150
Chicago, IL 60601
phone: (800) 586-4872
website: www.lung.org

More than one hundred years old, the American Lung Association is dedicated to preserving the lung health of all Americans. Its website offers information on tobacco products, the health effects of smoking, how lungs work, and what grade states earn on tobacco prevention, access to smoke cessation programs, and other criteria.

Campaign for Tobacco-Free Kids

1400 I St. NW, Suite 1200
Washington, DC 20005
phone: (202) 296-5469
website: www.tobaccofreekids.org

The Campaign for Tobacco-Free Kids is a nonprofit group that advocates for public policies that prevent young people from smoking and exposes Big Tobacco's marketing tricks. The organization sponsors Kick Butts Day in March and encourages teens to post selfies stating that they are not replacements for smokers who have died.

Scene Smoking

909 12th St.
Sacramento, CA 95814
phone: (916) 444-5900
website: www.scenesmoking.org

Scene Smoking is run by Breathe California of Sacramento-Emigrant Trails, a local organization devoted to issues pertaining to clean air and the elimination of the unhealthy effects of tobacco. Scene Smoking offers the largest database of movie reviews based solely on smoking content.

US Food and Drug Administration

10903 New Hampshire Ave.
Silver Spring, MD 20993
phone: (888) 463-6332
website: www.fda.org

The US Food and Drug Administration is the federal agency whose Center for Tobacco Products is responsible for carrying out the Tobacco Control Act. By following the website's Tobacco Products link visitors can learn more about the Tobacco Control Act and the FDA's youth and tobacco initiatives.

For Further Research

Books
Michael Eriksen, Judith Mackay, and Hana Ross, *The Tobacco Atlas*. Atlanta, GA: American Cancer Society, 2012.

Roman Espejo, *Tobacco and Smoking: Opposing Viewpoints*. Farmington Hills, MI: Greenhaven, 2015.

Mimi Nichter, *Lighting Up: The Rise of Social Smoking on College Campuses*. New York: New York University Press, 2015.

Stephanie Paris, *Straight Talk: Smoking*. Huntington Beach, CA: Teacher Created Materials, 2012.

Anthony Rebuck, *Breathing Poison: Smoking, Pollution and the Haze*. Bloomington, IN: Author Solutions, 2014.

Internet Sources
Kathryn Doyle, "Smoking Tied to Changes In the Structure of Teen Brains," *Reuters Health*, March 3, 2014. www.reuters.com/article/2014/03/03/us-smoking-brain-idUSBREA221W020140303.

Rachel Feltman, "1 in 5 Teens Smoke Hookah; Half Think It's Healthful," *Washington Post*, July 10, 2014. www.washingtonpost.com/news/to-your-health/wp/2014/07/10/1-in-5-teens-smoke-hookah-half-think-its-healthful.

Fresh Air, "Why Teens Are Impulsive, Addiction-Prone and Should Protect Their Brains," January 28, 2015. www.npr.org/blogs/health/2015/01/28/381622350/why-teens-are-impulsive-addiction-prone-and-should-protect-their-brains.

Abigail Jones, "Making Menthol Uncool," *Newsweek Global*, April 18, 2014. www.newsweek.com/2014/04/18/making-menthol-uncool-248123.html.

Alexandra Sifferlin, "Teen Smoking Is Way Down. But What About E-Cigs?," *Time*, June 12, 2014. http://time.com/2864214 /teen-smoking-is-way-down-but-what-about-e-cigs.

Websites

In The Mix: The Truth Unfiltered (www.pbs.org/inthemix /shows/show_smoking.html). Companion website to the 1998 PBS documentary about how tobacco companies marketed cigarettes to young smokers. Visitors to the website can follow a link to a transcript of a conversation among several teens with Jamie Ostroff of Memorial Sloan-Kettering Cancer Center in New York City in which they discuss their tobacco use.

Monitoring the Future (www.monitoringthefuture.org). Monitoring the Future is an ongoing study of the behaviors, attitudes, and values of secondary school students, college students, and young adults. Visitors to the website can check out the latest survey results and trends regarding middle school students and learn which brands of cigarettes are the most popular among teenagers.

Tips from Former Smokers (www.cdc.gov/tobacco/cam paign/tips). The Centers for Disease Control and Prevention's website for its antismoking campaign, Tips from Former Smokers allows visitors to watch videos illustrating the price real people have paid for smoking. Facts about tobacco, e-cigarettes, and proposed new FDA regulations on tobacco can also be accessed.

Truth (www.thetruth.com). Official website of the antismoking campaign Truth, whose purpose is to end smoking forever. Visitors to the website can watch the latest antismoking video, view poll results, learn specific ways they can join the movement, and view the movement's progress.

US Surgeon General (www.surgeongeneral.gov). The website of the nation's leading spokesperson on health matters features an entire section on tobacco that offers fact sheets on smoking and youth and other specific demographics, as well as videos and podcasts reflecting the progress made in reducing smoking in the five decades that have followed the surgeon general's declaration that smoking is bad for human health.

Videos

Ryan Au. "What Smoking Really Does to the Lungs After Just 60 Cigarettes." Online video. *YouTube*. May 23, 2014. www .youtube.com/watch?v=tCdOAzyKplM.

Food and Drug Administration. "Your Teeth: Real Cost Commercial." Online video. *YouTube*. February 4, 2014. www.you tube.com/watch?v=Ks2L6XFLAeA.

Truth. "Left Swipe Dat Official Music Video." Online video. *YouTube*. February 4, 2015. www.youtube.com/watch?v=fc Aj3lOyv3s.

Index

Picture Credits

Cover: Thinkstock Images

Radu Bercan/Shutterstock: 62

© David Bro/Zuma Press/Corbis: 57

ChameleonsEye/Shutterstock: 42

Depositphotos: 48

Simon Fraser/Science Source: 39

Laborant/Shutterstock: 15

Photofest Images: 33

John Powell/REX/Newscom: 6

Jon-Michael Sullivan/Zuma Press/Newscom: 53

Thinkstock Images: 11, 19, 25

© Dennis Van Tine/Retna Ltd./Corbis: 29

Gail Snyder is a freelance writer and advertising copywriter who has written nearly twenty books for young readers. She lives in Chalfont, Pennsylvania, with her husband, Hal Marcovitz.

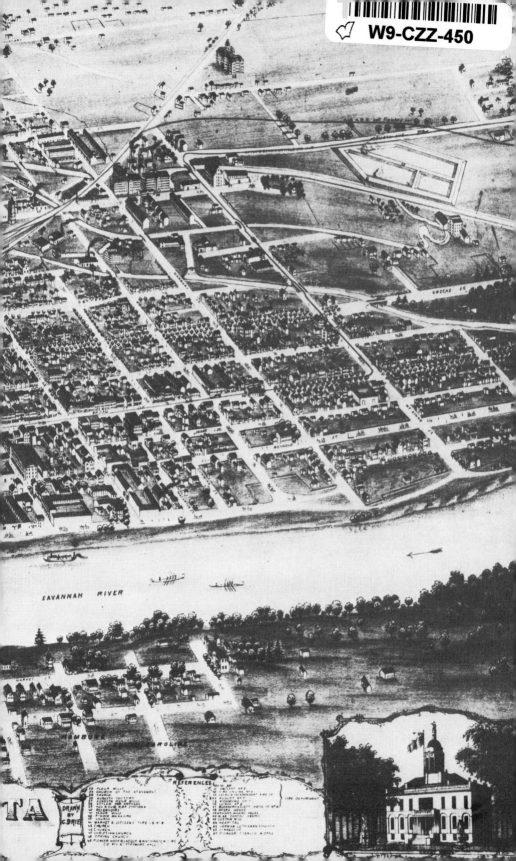

Yesterday's Augusta

Dear "Bill",

Congratulations on your graduation from Medical College.

Best of luck and good fortune to you in the future.

May you have good memories of Augusta, Ga. and the "old" lady neighbor on Beaufort Drive.

Much happiness always,
With love,
Myrtle Herron

June 5, 1982

Seemann's Historic Cities Series

A. RAY ROWLAND & HELEN CALLAHAN

Yesterday's

AUGUSTA

Seemann's Historic Cities Series No. 27

E. A. SEEMANN PUBLISHING, INC.
Miami, Florida

A number of individuals and institutions kindly provided pictures and other information for this book. Their contributions, credited in abbreviated form at the end of each caption, are gratefully acknowledged:

AC	Augusta College Library
APL	Augusta Richmond County Public Library
Anderson	Mr. and Mrs. Daniel L. Anderson, Belvedere, South Carolina
C of C	Chamber of Commerce of Greater Augusta
Callahan	The Callahan Family Collection, Augusta
Craven	Mrs. V. Jack Craven, Augusta
DAR	Daughters of the American Revolution, Augusta
Fair	Mr. and Mrs. William Eve Fair, Jr., Augusta
Godin	Mr. and Mrs. Jules Godin, Augusta
Harrison	Mr. and Mrs. D. Landrum Harrison, Augusta
McKenzie	Miss Myrtis McKenzie, Augusta
Marschalk	Dr. F. F. Marschalk, Augusta
Mulherin	Miss Louise Mulherin, Augusta
Pfadenhauer	Mrs. Ruby Mabry McCrary Pfadenhauer, Augusta
RCHS	Richmond County Historical Society
Richardson	Mrs. C. M. Richardson, Augusta
Reid	Reid Memorial Presbyterian Church, Augusta
St. Joseph's	Saint Joseph's Hospital, Augusta
St. Paul's	Saint Paul's Episcopal Church, Augusta
Schweers	Sister Rose Margaret Schweers, C.S.J., Augusta
Sheehan	Miss Anna Sheehan, Augusta
Stewart	Alice F. Stewart Collection, Augusta
Stulb	The Charles C. Stulb Family Collection, North Augusta, South Carolina
Thomas	Mr. and Mrs. Arthur Thomas, Jr., Augusta
Tommins	The Tommins Family Collection, Augusta
University Hospital	University Hospital, Augusta
Weigle	Mr. and Mrs. John Weigle, Augusta

Contents

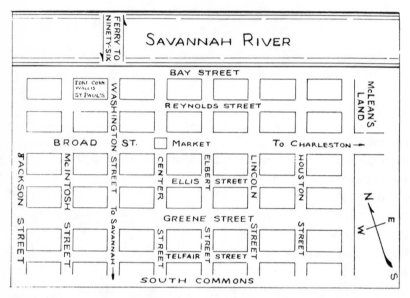

THIS PLAN was laid out in 1780 by commissioners William Glascock, Daniel McMurphy, John Twiggs, George Walton, and George Wells. The named streets running north-south have also been numbered. Houston is Second; Lincoln is Third; Elbert, Fourth; Center, Fifth; Washington, Sixth; McIntosh, Seventh; and Jackson, Eighth. (RCHS)

[6]

Preface

FORTY YEARS AGO, Augusta celebrated its bicentennial with ceremonies and pageantry which are still remembered by many citizens. As we commemorate the nation's bicentennial, it is appropriate to review again the life of this community as the town progressed from a Georgia backcountry trading post to one of the largest metropolitan areas of the state.

This book attempts to give a pictorial view of Georgia's second oldest city. It is unfortunate that numerous fires and floods have destroyed so much of Augusta's history. The loss of some pictures has prevented giving the full story of the city that we would have liked; nevertheless, many individuals managed to save materials which have been useful in preparing this volume.

Obviously, we have made no attempt to write a definitive history of Augusta. Rather, by presenting a selection of pictures, we hinted at what life was like in the community for over a hundred years. Since landmarks also were lost during the numerous disasters over the years, some scenes will be totally unfamiliar to younger Augustans and new residents, but many natives will be able to reach back in memory to those former places and events. Additionally, in recent years many buildings have been remodeled or torn down in the name of progress. We have included several examples of this progress—most noticeable in the changing face of Broad Street. Ironically, the current "downtown revitalization project" will restore one of the most attractive features of our main thoroughfare's past—trees will once more beautify the business sector.

Mrs. Daniel L. Anderson furnished a treasure house of the early flood and fires with the pictures that her husband rescued from a trash bin. Her interest in everything historical has been instrumental in preserving some of the most valuable pictures appearing in the book.

[7]

The basic collection of pictures which generated the idea for his book came from the files of the Richmond County Historical Society. Even though the Society was not founded until 1946, Mrs. Mary Carter Winter, its founder, president, and a long-time newspaper writer, was able to collect and preserve a valuable core of materials concerning the city. Still we would have lost part of the story without the help of Mr. Roscoe Williams, Assistant Dean of Students at Augusta College and photographer extraordinary, who reproduced pictures from old negatives and illustrations from several rare publications.

Mary A. Craven has assisted in many ways in the preparation of this project. Not only was she helpful in identifying pictures, but she also helped correct mistakes, and assisted with the typing and preparation of the finished manuscript. Her help during the past fifteen years has made one's job easier. Also, Oneida R. Gibson, Dell R. Rowland, and Kathleen Bone assisted with typing and many details. Without their assistance it would have been impossible to produce this book. Their help is greatly appreciated.

To Jane T. Rowland, whose patience enabled one of us to become over-involved, a special thanks. We are sincerely grateful to Nellie D. Callahan and Kathryn Callahan, who contacted possible contributors, collected pictures and albums, and added their enthusiasm to the project. Dr. Edward J. Cashin, Jr., Professor of History at Augusta College, read the manuscript and offered several helpful suggestions. His assistance is appreciated.

Arthur Ray Rowland
Helen Callahan

Augusta, Georgia
December 31, 1975

Trading Post to Textile Town: The Early History to 1870

NATURE SET THE COURSE for much of the colonial settlement of the Atlantic states millions of years ago. As the ocean receded eastward, the fall line of the rivers flowing from the mountains to the sea marked the limit of navigation. In addition, the slower currents below the falls provided safer crossings. In time along this line travel routes, trading posts, villages, and finally metropolitan areas developed. Augusta, Georgia, is one of the cities that followed this pattern.

Long before the British came up the Savannah River, the falls area had been a thriving Indian trading locale. Nor were these English colonists the first Europeans to penetrate this valley. In the spring of 1540, Hernando de Soto and his men camped several days at Silver Bluff, southeast of present-day Augusta, while they explored the region, traded with the friendly Indians, and pilfered local burial mounds.

In the later seventeenth and early eighteenth centuries, white trappers and traders passed through the area heading deeper into the piedmont seeking furs to be sold for a considerable profit at the colonial sea ports. Some merchants, such as Kennedy O'Brien, recognized that this long-established trade route could be exploited more fully if a trading post and warehouse were built beside the river. But if there ever was a definite plan to develop an independent commercial settlement, it was negated by the official decision to erect a frontier post under the authority of the Trustees for establishing the Colony of Georgia.

Since its formal beginning in 1735, Augusta's growth has been influenced by the river, the military, trade, and later, cotton. Only two years after James Edward Oglethorpe founded the colony of Georgia at Savannah, he sent a detachment of troops up the Savannah River and ordered that a town be built

[9]

PRINCESS AUGUSTA OF SAXE-GOTHA (1719-1772) was the wife of Frederick, Prince of Wales, and the mother of King George III. Augusta was named for her. The portrait was painted by C. Phillips in 1736. (AC)

on the right bank at the head of navigation. The new settlement was to serve the dual purpose of capturing the lucrative Indian fur trade and providing a first line of defense against Spanish, French, or Indian attacks upon English pioneers. Oglethorpe named the town in honor of Princess Augusta, the wife of Frederick, Prince of Wales, and the mother of the future King George III.

Each spring the town thronged with hundreds of Indian traders who gathered to send their furs downriver to the coast. Large barges carried the skins to the port at Savannah and returned loaded with goods used in bartering in the back country. To maintain this early prosperity, peace with the Indians had to be preserved. In 1739, Oglethorpe concluded a treaty of friendship and trade with several chiefs at Coweta Town, near present day Columbus, Georgia. On his return journey, the general became so ill that he stopped in Augusta to recuperate. This layover was Oglethorpe's only visit to the colony's second-oldest settlement.

Augusta was a typical frontier town. The hard-working and hard-living pioneers frequently preferred to settle their own disagreements without the services of the local magistrate. In 1740, the commander of Fort Augusta complained of the "jangling among the traders" and the extent to which violence was used to solve quarrels.

Since there was such concern for the morals and manners of the citizenry, the petition of Augustans in 1750 for a minister certainly must have gladdened the hearts of colonial officials in Savannah. The first Saint Paul's Church was a small wooden structure built next to the fort for protection. The enthusiasm of the first pastor, the Rev. Jonathan Copp, waned when he came to realize that of his congregation of nearly one hundred there were only eight communicants. The poor man became quite disillusioned when he discovered the true condition of the church glebe and learned that the construction of a parsonage was in the vague future. Obviously, Augustans had not mended their ways nearly as much as the colonial authorities had hoped.

While the fear of attack constantly existed in the community, feelings were especially tense during the French and Indian War, for the frontier area seemed assailable by French and Spanish troops and their Indian allies. After nearly thirty years as an outpost, Augustans were relieved and pleased to learn that the Peace of Paris in 1763 extended the boundaries of Georgia further inland. To explain to the Indians the territorial adjustments agreed upon by European powers, a conference was held in Augusta which was attended by colonial officials from Virginia, the Carolinas, and Georgia, and by chiefs from the major Indian nations and tribes of the affected region. As a result of the friendly discussions and negotiations conducted in 1763, the Indians ceded additional land to the colonists.

The new sense of security felt by Augustans was expressed in the physical and economic growth of the community. As the land around the town be-

THE ACADEMY of Richmond County, incorporated in 1783, moved to this new building on the south side of Telfair Street in 1802. (RCHS)

came more settled, the use of slave labor kept pace with the increasing acre-
age under cultivation. Augusta served as a market for agricultural products, a
trading post and warehouse for trappers, and a river port for merchants,
boatmen, and travelers. By the 1770s, the future of the area indeed appeared
destined for economic success. The Second Treaty of Augusta in 1773 seemed to assure the town's good fortune, for the Creek and Cherokee nations
ceded 2,000,000 acres northwest of Augusta. Within a year, however, Indian
attacks occurred in the ceded lands.

    This renewed threat was reflected in the attitude of Augustans toward the

MEADOW GARDEN, built in the latter part of the eighteenth century, became the post-
revolutionary home of George Walton, a signer of the Declaration of Independence and
an early governor of Georgia. With the construction of the canal during the nineteenth
century, the vicinity around Meadow Garden was transformed from a peaceful, suburban
neighborhood into a manufacturing area. (RCHS)

THE FORMER HOME of Dr. Paul Fitzsimmons Eve stands at 619 Greene Street. The house, a two-story attic frame built on a high brick basement, was erected in 1814. Dr. Eve was one of the founders of the Medical College and distinguished himself as a surgeon in the Polish Revolution of 1830. (C of C)

AUGUSTANS DELAYED connecting the rail lines on the Georgia side of the Savannah with the South Carolina Railway Company for over ten years. The city fathers argued that such a union would cause Augusta to become merely a line town rather than a depot and commercial center. Draymen, quite satisfied with the income to be gained from transporting goods across the river between Augusta and Hamburg, supported the status quo. But in 1852, Charleston threatened to negotiate a river crossing for the South Carolina Railway elsewhere. Faced with the possibility of being bypassed, Augusta withdrew its objection to the railroad bridge and the South Carolina Company crossed the Savannah River in 1853. (RCHS)

[13]

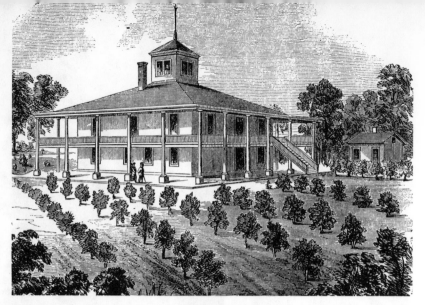

THE BERCKMANS PLANTATION was one of the largest nurseries in the South. Prosper J. A. Berckmans, a Belgian, and his sons worked here not only as horticulturists but also as landscape architects. Many of the more than eighty men who were employed at the Fruitland Nurseries were provided living quarters on the property. Wide varieties of flowers, plants, shrubs, and trees were raised at Fruitland Nurseries. The Berckmans plantation house later became the clubhouse of the Augusta National. (RCHS)

tense situations developing elsewhere between the colonies and England. Naturally, the colonial disputes and grumblings against recent Parliamentary actions were known locally, but Augustans did not become involved. Georgia held a unique position in its relationship with England. Of all the colonies, it was the only settlement instigated and supported by the British government. Loyalty ties were strong for many Georgians. But probably more important to the local citizens was their vulnerability to Indian raids if British aid and protection were removed. Nevertheless, after the Battles of Lexington, Concord, and Breed's Hill, a group of "Liberty Boys" began to operate in the Augusta area. Yet, the fear of Indian attacks remained paramount. When an ad hoc provisional council was set up in Savannah after the signing of the Declaration of Independence, one of the first communiques that it received was from Augusta requesting increased defenses.

In 1777, Georgia adopted a constitution. Under the new political structure, counties replaced the former parishes. Richmond County, named after the Duke of Richmond, a spokesman in Parliament for the American position, replaced Saint Paul's Parish, and Augusta became the county seat.

During the American Revolution, Georgians not only fought the British for physical control of the state but struggled among themselves to gain its political power. When Savannah fell to the British on December 28, 1778, Augusta became the state capital. But by January 31, Lt. Col. Archibald

Campbell, leading British forces, marched into Augusta. This first occupation was short-lived, for as American troops continued to gather across the river in South Carolina, Campbell decided to withdraw. Augusta again became the seat of the state government. But peace for the area was not yet to be realized. While the British still held the coast, political bickering in Augusta grew to such proportions that one Georgian wrote, ". . . Augusta is now. . . the Residence of many worthy men, but the Receptacle also of some of those pests to society who will eternally mar every virtuous undertaking. . . ."

British troops under the command of Lt. Col. Thomas Brown, who in 1775 as an Augusta resident had been tarred and feathered by local "Liberty Boys," captured Augusta again in June 1780. Although American forces led by Col. Elijah Clark attempted to rescue the city in September, the siege failed. The British continued their occupation for the next nine months. Then on June 5, 1781, after a struggle that lasted over two weeks, Brown and his garrison surrendered to Lt. Col. Henry Lee.

The war was over for Augustans who began to rebuild their battle-scarred community. In 1783, the Georgia Legislature appointed five Trustees of Richmond Academy to lay out the town, sell specific public lands, operate a ferry, reconstruct Saint Paul's Church, and establish a "seminary of learning." The grid pattern for the town design actually complied with the plan that Ogle- [15]

THE CITY MARKET was demolished by a cyclone in February 1878. The building, which stood in the middle of Broad at Center (Fifth) Street, had replaced an earlier market that had burned in April 1829. Often referred to as the "Slave Market," it was the center of activities other than the slave auctions held the first of each month. Inside the building were butcher stalls, meat shops, poultry coops, and stands for vegetables, fruit, and dairy products. Farm animals and pets could be purchased behind the building. The market also acted as an "information center" for Augustans and Savannah River area farmers—the latest news was spread, political issues debated, gentleman's agreements made, gossip swapped, and advice, sought or unwanted, given. When the market was destroyed in 1878, one column remained standing. Local legend states that harm will come to anyone who attempts to remove "The Haunted Pillar." (RCHS)

WOODROW WILSON spent his boyhood in this home at Telfair and McIntosh (Seventh) streets, while his father, the Rev. Dr. Joseph R. Wilson, was minister of the First Presbyterian Church from 1858 to 1870. One of President Wilson's first memories was the excitement in Augusta when word was received that Abraham Lincoln had been elected. When war came, Dr. Wilson was active locally in supporting the Confederacy. This picture, taken in the twentieth century, shows the house unchanged. (C of C)

thorpe had drawn up earlier for Augusta, but over the years the buildings and residences had become scattered along the main road.

The Academy of Richmond County opened in 1785, as part of the state university system chartered that year. The first academy was situated near the river on Bay Street between Lincoln (3rd) and Elbert (4th) Streets. George Washington, during his visit to the city in 1791, attended oral examinations at the school. By 1802 larger quarters were necessary. The new Richmond Academy on Telfair between Center (5th) and Washington (6th) was constructed with hand-made, stucco-covered brick. For 124 years, this building housed one of the finest and most famous academies in Georgia. The 500 block of Telfair became somewhat of an educational center. In 1834, construction of the Medical College, which had been authorized six years earlier, began on the Washington Street corner. Until 1911, the two institutions operated side by side, sometimes exchanging faculty members for special lectures or courses. When the Medical College moved, Richmond Academy took over the building for its science department and manual training classes. Despite the addition of the old medical facility and the temporary use of rooms across the street in the Court House, Richmond Academy still needed more space. In 1926, the Academy and the newly authorized Junior College of Augusta moved into a new building on Baker Avenue just off Walton Way.

The Augusta Arsenal also began as a riverside establishment that later was located on what became Walton Way. Authorized by the United States government three years earlier, the Augusta Arsenal opened in 1819 in the vicinity of the current King Mill. Disaster struck the garrison within a year; the troops except for two officers died of swamp fever. Although the post commander, Capt. H. M. Payne, was stricken also, he was taken to Bellevue Plantation on "the Hill," where he regained his health. The other survivor was on leave at the time of the epidemic. Captain Payne's recovery led to the belief that Bellevue was a more healthful location than the river site. When it became known that the government planned to purchase the plantation to relocate the arsenal, the residents of the nearby village of Summerville voiced strong opposition. Local opinion changed to favor the project, however, when the federal authorities intimated that if the civilians were so opposed to the military in their midst then they would transfer the entire post to another city. To some Augustans, the presence of a military garrison meant protection against possible slave uprisings as well as an additional financial asset for the

THE OGLETHORPE INFANTRY, Augusta's oldest volunteer unit, was organized in 1850. During the state military convention held in late 1860, the Oglethorpes took a conservative position opposing secession; when Georgia seceded, however, the company immediately offered its services to Gov. Joseph E. Brown. The regiment's first assignment was the defense of Fort Pickens at Pensacola, Florida. (RCHS)

THE RICHMOND HUSSARS, Augusta's cavalrymen, were organized in 1855. Since each volunteer had to furnish his own horse, equipment, and weapons, membership in the unit tended to be selective. The Hussars entertained spectators at their exercises by staging cavalry charges, conducting target practice at full gallop, and engaging in sabre drills. Following the fall of Fort Sumter, Capt. Thomas S. Stovall volunteered their services to the Confederacy, and the Hussars joined Thomas R. R. Cobb's command. (RCHS)

community. Seventy-two acres of land were purchased in 1826, and construction of the Augusta Arsenal began the following year. For over 125 years, this facility manufactured and stored arms and munitions. When the arsenal was closed after the Korean War, a portion of the property was acquired for the Junior College of Augusta. Since the college moved to the site in 1957, additional sections of the old arsenal have been purchased for the expanding educational institution.

In addition to the military, the river and trade had always been prominent influences on the life of Augusta. Both of these factors became particularly important once cotton began to dominate the local market. In 1793 Eli Whitney invented the cotton gin, which was so simple to operate that the machine was easily duplicated. Before long, gins were in operation throughout the South.

Augusta's location in the cotton belt and on the Savannah River created a natural market area early in the 1800s. Wagons bearing the precious cargo rolled into the city where planters and cotton merchants haggled over fluctuating market prices. After the bargain had been struck, the bales were stored in the warehouses located along the river to await steam transportation to Savannah.

Railroad transportation was first introduced into the valley across the river. In 1833 the South Carolina Railway Company completed the Charleston-Hamburg line. Shortly thereafter, during that same year, the Georgia Railroad Company was chartered and began construction, employing many of the experienced Irish laborers who had laid track for the South Carolina line. When the railroads linked middle Georgia to the city in the early 1840s, Augusta gained even more importance as a cotton trade center.

Since there were great quantities of cotton available locally, it became evident to some businessmen that the city possessed the potential to become a great textile center. The successful use of water power from several county streams convinced Henry H. Cumming, Nicholas De Laigle, James Fraser, John P. King, and Andrew J. Miller that the power of the Savannah River could be utilized for industrial purposes by a canal system.

Authorized by a city ordinance in 1845, the Augusta Canal was completed two years later. Although the Augusta Manufacturing Company, one of the first industries to take advantage of this source of power, floundered after a few years, local enthusiasm for using the canal for manufacturing remained strong. Incorporated in 1859, the Augusta Factory absorbed the old plant and soon converted it into a highly successful textile operation.

Though still a small town by today's standards, Augusta in 1860 had a population of 12,493 and was one of Georgia's largest cities. As the presidential election of that crucial year approached, some Augusta citizens spoke out voicing their wish that the North should leave the South alone to handle its

[19]

THE CLINCH RIFLES are being reviewed by Capt. C. A. Platt on the parade ground in front of the Augusta Arsenal in 1861. The Georgia flag with one star is flying between the commandant's house and the headquarters building. (RCHS)

WILLIAM H. GOODRICH operated a sash, door, and blind factory at 187 Reynolds Street in the 1860s and 1870s. Starting out in the early 1840s as a carpenter, Mr. Goodrich built a large, successful business. (RCHS)

own problems, especially as they related to slavery. After Abraham Lincoln was elected president in November, Augustans were not of a single opinion, but there was already talk of secession and war. Not only were many individuals advocating this stance, but several military units were anxious to take up arms immediately. When the news of South Carolina's secession from the Union on December 20, 1860, reached the city, Mayor Foster Blodgett called a town meeting at City Hall to discuss the South Carolina stand. The sentiment of the moderates prevailed at this gathering, but the secessionists met separately and passed a resolution which was presented to the legislature as the official position of the citizens of Augusta and Richmond County. Augustans did unite later, and in the election held for local officials on January 5, 1861, all the candidates advocating immediate secession were elected. Even as the talk of living as a divided union went on, Augusta and the rest of the Confederacy began preparation for war.

Of immediate concern was the presence of federal troops at the United States Arsenal on the outskirts of Augusta. Even though they were isolated, for a few days life at the Arsenal went on as usual. To avoid a clash, if possible, Gov. Joseph Brown personally came to Augusta to take possession of the Arsenal in the name of the state. After an uneasy negotiation, with 800 soldiers from various local units standing by, Capt. Arnold Elzey surrendered to Governor Brown on January 24, 1861. In accord with the terms, the store of arms was left, and the federal troops were assured safe passage to New York. The surrender was friendly, and the federal troops and local militia visited each other during the days while passage by way of Savannah was being arranged. "The Battle of Augusta" was over; the surrender took place without the firing of a single shot. While this easy victory was deceptive in some ways, it was indicative of how Augusta would be untouched by the cannon balls and mortar fire of a shooting battle.

Mobilization activities were everywhere. Many Augusta and Richmond County boys donned the Confederate grey and became "Johnny Rebs," as company after company left for duty in Florida, Virginia, and throughout the Confederacy. Before the war was ended, two thousand had left for the battle-fields. Of these, 292 were killed or died in service.

In spite of shortages, the war generally brought prosperity to the city. The cotton mills and other factories produced many essentials for the Confederacy. The Augusta Factory, one of the largest textile mills in the South, produced an average of 20,000 yards of cloth a day, most of which was sold to the government.

The Confederate pistol factory eventually settled in Augusta after it had been driven from city after city by the invading Union forces. By 1863, the Confederate government was establishing factories of its own as existing plants operated by private enterprise could not supply its needs. Augusta became a center for the clothing needed by the soldiers. Confederate uniforms made locally kept 1,500 women busy sewing. The city had a shoe factory, served as a food supply center, and was a primary rail center for much of the supplies from this section of the South.

Yet, the most significant war efforts in Augusta were the expansion of the

[21]

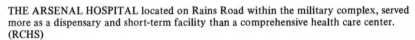

THE ARSENAL HOSPITAL located on Rains Road within the military complex, served more as a dispensary and short-term facility than a comprehensive health care center. (RCHS)

arsenal and the establishment of the Confederate Powder Works under the command of George Washington Rains. The powder works, one of the largest in the world, was housed in buildings extending two miles along the Augusta Canal. In its three years of existence, the plant manufactured 2,750,000 pounds of gunpowder. The deep sentiment for the Southern cause was evident when church bells from New Orleans, Charleston, Savannah, Augusta, and other Southern cities were melted down and made into four brass cannons at the Augusta Arsenal. By 1863, the city had become one of the major military supply sources for the Army.

While the activities at the arsenal and powder works expanded, Augusta also became a medical center. Originally serving only as a hospital for wounded soldiers passing through, more and more men were sent to Augusta for treatment as the war progressed. The Presbyterian, Saint Patrick's Catholic, Saint John Methodist, and Saint Paul's Episcopal churches were used as hospitals. The Sisters of Mercy and the ladies of the city volunteered for nursing duties. As the multitude of those requiring care increased, so did the need for more food and supplies. Citizens strained to provide resources, and shortages became even greater.

In North Georgia, William Tecumseh Sherman had destroyed Atlanta and began his march through the state by November 1865. At the time, it seemed obvious that Augusta with its vast powder works and as a military supply center would be one of his targets. By Thanksgiving, thousands of Augustans were digging fortifications around the city, while ten thousand troops from Wilmington under the command of Gen. Braxton Bragg arrived as reinforcements. Sherman's march continued to the sea, but the general bypassed Augusta to take Savannah on December 25, 1865. Augusta fortified itself a second time when Sherman left the Coast. By February 8, 1865, however, it was again evident that the city was not going to be Sherman's target as his troops advanced on Columbia. By cutting off the two armies of the Confederacy from its supply center at Augusta, there was no need to destroy the city. Its factories and powder works were lost to Southern armies.

Locally, the war ended May 3, 1865, when Brevet Maj. Gen. Emory Upton of the United States Army came to the city to receive the surrender of the arsenal from Capt. W. H. Warren, acting for Colonel Rains. Federal forces occupied the city, and Maj. Gen. John Pope established military rule for the first time in Augusta's history. In spite of the financial difficulties facing everyone after the fall of the Confederacy, the Georgia Railroad transported home free more than 100,000 paroled Confederate prisoners. By 1868, reconstruction and military rule were ended, and Henry R. Russell was elected mayor. In 1869, he was succeeded by J. V. H. Allen, who brought discipline and order to the city through the reorganization of the police force.

Building on the Past: 1870 to 1900

THE YEARS of the Civil War and Reconstruction were only an interlude in Augusta's progress. Earlier industrial development had prepared a solid basis to which the city could return easily in the postwar period. Augusta, after the Civil War, was little changed. There were no battle damages, and the city was under the control of the Reconstruction government only for a short time. The period from 1870 to 1900 was marked by a rapid industrial growth.

Several factors contributed to this progress. When the city acquired the site of the Confederate Powder Works in 1872, local civic leaders anticipated that it would develop into a manufacturing complex. The enlargement of the Augusta Canal in 1875 during the administration of Mayor Charles Estes, however, was the major factor that led to the building of several new cotton mills. The availability of a large amount of capital, both from northern and local sources, an abundant supply of cheap labor, and the necessary power to operate the mills thrust Augusta into an industrial expansion much ahead of other cities of comparable size. The organization of the Enterprise Factory in 1872, the Sibley Manufacturing Company in 1880, and the John P. King Manufacturing Company in 1882, boosted an already growing textile industry and provided profits and dividends that ranged from 18 to 24 percent. Between 1880 and 1890, manufacturing in Augusta increased 580 percent—leading the South in percentage of increase.

Not only did the cotton mills flourish, but they gave rise to a number of supportive industries and related services. The railroads expanded to ship the manufactured products, and several foundries provided the parts to keep the machinery in operation. All of this raised the number and buying power of local wage earners who frequented the thriving mercantile establishments on Broad and connecting streets.

[23]

FACULTY AND STUDENTS of the Medical College gather on the steps of the original
school building designed by C. C. Clusky in 1835. The classic style is beautifully and
simply displayed in the six massive Greek Doric columns which support the pediment.
Located on the corner of Telfair and Washington (Sixth) streets, the building was used
by the Medical College until the school moved to the former Tuttle-Newton Home at
Railroad Avenue and Harper Street in 1911. Note the railroad tracks which still run
through the center of the city. (RCHS)

The composition of Augusta's population changed during the last decades
of the nineteenth century. European and Asian immigrants, workers from
abandoned farms, and former slaves came to find work in the city. The
Chinese, who were brought to Augusta as laborers for the canal enlargement
project, remained to become owners and operators of laundries, groceries,
and restaurants before the century ended.

It was also during this period that several distinctive neighborhoods developed. Since the Georgia Railroad was their principal employer, the Irish chose
to live near their place of work, and set up their residences south of the
railroad yards in the area that became known as Dublin. The blacks also
settled on the south side of the railroad tracks in the section called the Terri.
While they were mostly employed as unskilled laborers and domestic servants,
a few blacks held jobs with the Georgia Railroad, the Augusta Brick Company, and the Georgia Chemical Company.

Another famous neighborhood was Harrisburg, where a large number of
the mill workers settled. Intensely proud Harrisburgers claimed Hawk's
Gulley (15th Street) and the King Mill Bridge as their boundaries. Generally,
the mill people did not feel oppressed and were happy people. One worker
remembered thinking that the factory was a large beautiful place of machinery.

[24]

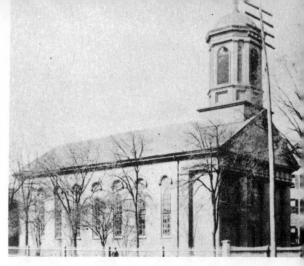

THE ORIGINAL FIRST BAPTIST Church was built in 1821 on the corner of Greene and Jackson (Eighth) streets, the location of a former racetrack. Four years earlier a group of local Baptists organized the Baptist Praying Society of Augusta and set themselves the task of raising funds for a church building. In 1845, the Southern Baptist Convention was organized in this church. A new building replaced the old structure in 1902. (RCHS)

The disillusionment of the workers with the failure of wages to keep pace with rising prices eventually led to dark clouds on the normally good relationship between management and labor. The eruption of the Knights of Labor strikes in 1886 and again in 1898-1899 caused the mills temporarily to close their doors. Since the management did not concede, the union eventually met defeat. Except for this attempt to break the power of the industrial establishment, Augusta enjoyed industrial growth and prosperity.

Beyond the principal downtown residential areas, the suburban areas of Summerville, Monte Sano, and across the river North Augusta, South Carolina, were beginning to develop. The first streetcar lines to the Hill were completed as Augusta moved into the era of becoming truly urban.

[25]

J. B. WHITE AND COMPANY first opened its doors in Augusta in 1874 and has remained a leading department store despite suffering severe damage on several occasions from floods and near total destruction in the 1921 fire. (Anderson)

THE CONFEDERATE SECTION of Magnolia Cemetery ramains a monument to those who died in the service of their country. Each Memorial Day, a ceremony honoring their sacrifice is held. In years gone by, those attending the memorial service adjourned to neighboring May Park for a picnic. (RCHS)

[26]   SUMMERTIME IN AUGUSTA meant gathering under the shade trees, church picnics, family reunions, and birthday or anniversary celebrations. Directly south of Augusta, four generations take a pause from their day's activities in 1885 to pose for the traditional picture-taking. (RCHS)

SAINT JAMES METHODIST CHURCH erected this building in 1886 which has been described as a Southern adaption of classic Gothic architecture. Located at 439 Greene Street, the church was the second Methodist congregation organized in the city. (AC)

THE AUGUSTA EXCHANGE BUILDING, constructed in 1887, was the focal point of the city's commercial activities. Because of its location on Cotton Row, and the importance of that staple to the Savannah River area, the facility was usually referred to as the Cotton Exchange. Originally established in 1872, the exchange furnished Augusta's businessmen with the daily market prices from major cotton depots in the United States and England, grain and cattle quotations from Chicago, and the New York stock averages. (RCHS)

THE EXPOSITION BUILDING occupied part of the grounds of Druid Park. The exhibition hall was built in 1888 for a national exposition to publicize Augusta's natural and industrial advantages. Workmen can be seen clearing the tracks of the two electric car lines that ran in front of the great hall. Despite the disastrous flood of 1888 which postponed the opening for a month, the exposition was a success. The Augusta Exposition of 1891, however, was considered the greatest in number and variety of exhibits as well as profits realized. The building and grounds were also used for state and local fairs. The Gilbert-Lambuth Memorial Chapel of Paine College is now partially situated where the famous hall formerly stood. (RCHS)

THE ORIGINAL BON AIR HOTEL opened in 1889, signaling the beginning of Augusta as a winter resort. Destroyed by fire in 1920, this building was replaced by the present Bon Air Hotel. (RCHS)

[28]

COTTON WAS KING, and cotton pickers made the abundant harvest possible in the 1890s. Augusta and the surrounding area had vast cotton fields. Following the Civil War, many pickers continued to live and work on the plantations as tenant laborers. (APL)

THE OLD FOURTH WARD SCHOOL included grades one through seven. Here students and their teachers gathered in front of the building for a picture in 1888. (Richardson)

THE ARSENAL in the late nineteenth century was surrounded with a wooden fence. This picture, taken looking toward the guardhouse at the corner of Walton Way and Katherine Street, shows some of the older guns and stacks of cannon balls. (Pfadenhauer)

GREENE STREET, looking east from the bell tower as it appeared in the early 1890s: The steeple of the First Christian Church at Greene and McIntosh (Seventh) streets can be seen in the background. Mrs. Emily Tubman, a leading member of the church, helped finance its construction in 1876. (RCHS)

DANIEL O'LEARY and J. N. Walsh pose on the 700 block of Broad Street. The Commercial Club building can be seen behind the fenced Confederate Monument. (RCHS)

STUDENTS OF Richmond Academy posed on the step of the school in 1892, when knickers and high-top shoes were fashionable attire for the young man. The schoolmates were bottom row, left to right: Jim Parks, Arnold Kahrs, Charles Vaughn, Lamar Quillian, ___ Berry, A. Jones, Frank Dunbar, John E. Murphey, Robert Hahn, and William Quillan; middle row: Cortez Andrews, Dessie Miller, Joe Palmer, Bayard Caswell, Campbell Chaffee, Charles Hogrefe, Austin Daniel, B. S. Dunbar, Cleland Rood; top row: Charles Stafford, Charles Fesler, Chattie Oats, W. C. Pollard, Earle Barton, Gus White. (RCHS)

LOVERS' LANE extended southeastward from the railroad yards at East Boundary towards the river. A carriage ride down Lovers' Lane was a pleasant way to spend an afternoon in the gay 1890s. The road, however, led to an eerie drive when the river mists rose and fog settled over the area. (AC)

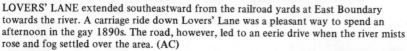

THE NEW CITY HOSPITAL, constructed in 1894 on the corner of Washington (Sixth) and Walker streets, cost the City Council of Augusta $39,000. At this institution Dr. W. H. Doughty, Jr., and Miss Anna David established the first local nurses' training school. Augusta's first City Hospital had been built on lower Greene Street between Forsyth (Second) and Houston (Third) streets. Then the City Council decided in 1869 that the facility would be better serviced if it were relocated behind the Medical College. The two-story frame building erected that year enlarged by a third-floor addition in 1881, served as a health care center until it was replaced in 1894 by the three-story brick new City Hospital built on the same site. (University Hospital)

HEADQUARTERS FOR THE FIRE Chief and the Chemical Engine No. 1 was located at the corner of Jones and Macartan streets. The chief's office had been moved to this site in 1851. Firemen are shown with their horse-drawn equipment while the chief and his assistant pose in the officers' buggy in 1895. The building now houses a clothing firm. (RCHS)

THE AUGUSTA FACTORY was incorporated in 1850, and by the 1890s, was manufacturing over thirteen million yards of cotton cloth a year. While the corporation's officers boasted of the production machinery—827 looms and 27,442 spindles—they were equally as proud of the company's management-labor relationship which they believed resulted from "capital working in harmony with a contented industrial population." Evidence of this cooperation included 111 homes for employees on the factory property, a nursery for working mothers, and a workers' sick and death benefits association. (RCHS)

[32]

THE NORTH AUGUSTA BRIDGE connecting Augusta with South Carolina at McKinne (Thirteenth) Street was built in 1891. During the 1908 flood, a section of the bridge was washed away. (AC)

[33]

SACRED HEART ACADEMY'S young ladies pose for their school picture in 1892. Bottom row, left to right: Daisy Gleason, Blanche Brooks, unknown, Georgia Costello, Cecile Durban, Annie Painter, Annie Lou Carr, Lena Baldowski, Sadie Campbell; second row, left to right: Annie Kate O'Connor, Parmie Austin, Lees Raworth, Circe Olofson, Mamie Wise, Emma Plunkett, Annie Lou Mosgrove, Addie Day, W. Lawrence, unknown, Marie Rudell, Maude Van Linge, Blanche Heffernan; third row, left to right: Rebecca Lattimore, Effie Neibling, Lucy Gray, unkown, unknown, unknown, Blanche Jordan; fourth row, left to right: Louisa Cain, Nora Baldowski, Emily Craig, Pauline Reubenstein, Annie Barren, Bessie Singleton, Maude Ray; and top row, left to right: unknown, Bessie Pague, unknown, Lumpkin Doughty, unknown, Katie Kidwell. (RCHS)

STORAGE SPACE for King Cotton was a valuable commodity, and pressing it into bales an important local business. In 1893, the Augusta Cotton and Compress Company could store nearly 5,000 bales of uncompressed cotton and over 8,000 bales of compressed cotton. The plant, located on Washington (Sixth) Street to take advantage of the railroad service could press 150 bales per hour. (AC)

BOARDINGHOUSES and family residences occupied the second and third floors over Broad Street business firms into the twentieth century. An enormous wisteria gave both beauty and fragrance to the northwestern corner of Broad and Macartan streets. (RCHS)

THESE TWO LATE-VICTORIAN-STYLE houses were built on the 1200 block of Ellis Street near the end of the nineteenth century. On a bleak winter afternoon in the 1890s, the residents posed on their porches, and a child perched on the gate post for the photographer. (RCHS)

THE RESIDENTIAL BLOCK of Broad Street west of McKinne (Thirteenth) Street shows the fine details of the late Victorian houses. (C of C)

PASSED DOWN to younger generations through the telling and retelling of the glories, the legends, the victories, and the defeats; sentiments for the "Lost Cause" were slow to fade. A group of young "Johnny Rebs" posed in the 1100 block of Greene Street in the late nineteenth century. (AC)

THE AUGUSTA FREE SCHOOL was founded in 1821 to provide an education for the poor of the community who could not afford tuition fees at local academies. Operation of the Augusta Free School was made possible through endowments and contributions. For over eighty years, it was located in the 700 block of Greene Street until the school moved to the 1200 block of D'Antignac in 1914, where it continued to function as a night school until it was abolished in 1916. (Anderson)

THE FIRST REID MEMORIAL PRESBYTERIAN CHURCH, erected in 1879 on the corner of Walton Way and Johns Road in the village of Summerville, was a gift of Robert A. Reid in memory of his wife Eleanor Louise Reid. Used in the beginning as a mission, the church soon attracted members from the downtown area as well as the Hill. Many of the city members of the congregation moved to Summerville and helped to establish the village as more than just a summer retreat for Augustans. (Reid)

ROWING ON THE AUGUSTA CANAL was a pleasant way to spend a few hours. It was even considered a safe diversion for young ladies to engage in alone. (Sheehan)

THE MANDOLIN GLEE CLUB, composed of prominent Augusta businessmen and physicians, provided local audiences with many pleasant musical evenings. Pictured in the bottom row, left to right: Dr. William A. Mulherin, Frank G. Bohler, Dessie Ford, Alec Edelblut, Dr. Robert H. Land; middle row, left to right: P. J. Rice, Dr. Thomas Vaughan, Joseph H. Mulherin, Leo Cotter, John P. Mulherin, Dan Bolster, John B. Murray, Tom Bresnahan, Tim Heffernan; back row, left to right: Ed Boulineau, unknown, John Hallinan, John Chapman, Thomas J. O'Leary, Dan P. O'Connor, Nichols, Thomas Bresnahan. (Mulherin)

SPANISH-AMERICAN WAR soldiers built a frame mess hall at Camp McKenzie in December 1898. (Pfadenhauer)

THE MEN of the 13th Pennsylvania Volunteers constructed a special company Christmas decoration at Camp McKenzie in 1898. (Pfadenhauer)

MULES of the 3rd Division pack train were readied for maneuvers at Camp McKenzie in February 1899. (Pfadenhauer)

THE TROOPS stationed at Camp McKenzie during the winter of 1898-99 experienced a rare occurrence for the Augusta area—a heavy snow fall. (Pfadenhauer)

Floods and Fires

DESPITE THE MANY ADVANTAGES of being a river town, Augusta was often the victim of the Savannah's raging waters. The captain of the garrison at Fort Augusta notified colonial officials in Savannah of flood damage in 1741, and ten years later the first pastor of Saint Paul's complained that the river overflowed once or twice a year. Since the Rev. Jonathan Copp was seeking a change of location for the church glebe, his accounts of the size and frequency of the high water incidents may have been exaggerated and intentionally vague. Yet, for over one hundred and fifty years flood disasters most certainly occurred periodically. Not until 1908 did protective measures begin to become reality, rather than a topic of temporary concern following a serious freshet.

In comparing the contemporary descriptions of the most severe floods (specifically 1796, 1840, 1852, 1865, 1887, 1888, and 1908), the main path of the rushing waters followed the old channel of the Beaver Dam Creek, which had flowed southeastwardly from the river about at the point of the present day Kollock (11th) Street. The Augusta Canal, completed in 1847, used sections of the old creek bed and, therefore, became a high water artery into the city. Spilling over the banks of this course, the floods spread into business and residential areas. Although the City Council discussed flood protection after the 1888 disaster which caused eleven deaths and $2,000,000 in damage, Augusta officials procrastinated. A bond referendum for construction of a levee was sought only after the 1908 disaster, which took eighteen lives and destroyed property valued at over $1,500,000. Even then, many Augustans bitterly opposed a city-wide bond issue of $1,000,000. Another high water in 1912 ended the dispute. Extending from the head gates of the Augusta Canal to Butler Creek, the levee was completed in 1915 at the cost

[39]

of $3,000,000, a fourth of which was financed by a federal grant. In 1928, the levee was strengthened and lengthened. Flood control for the Central Savannah River Area was assured by the completion of the Clark Hill Dam Project in the early 1950s.

Although the periodic submersion of the city had resulted in much loss of life and property over the years, the fire of 1916 was the worst disaster ever to befall Augusta. On March 22, 1916, at 6:20 p. m., fire broke out in Kelly's Dry Goods store, located in the Dyer Building, which stood at the northwest corner of Broad and Jackson (8th) streets, the present site of the First National Bank. Whipped on by high winds, the fire rapidly spread to other buildings on Broad and adjacent streets. In the wake of the flames, twenty-six blocks were totally destroyed, and seven more blocks partially demolished. The destruction of 138 businesses and 526 homes left more than 3,000 homeless and caused losses totaling over $10,000,000. Augusta's greatest

[40]

RESIDENTS of upper Reynolds Street had to be evacuated by boat as the waters rose in 1887. (Anderson)

DURING THE 1888 FLOODS, the railroad bridge across the river was battered and marred. Railroad men and volunteers saved the bridge by preventing the debris floating down the river from lodging against the structure. (Anderson)

disaster has been described as an unnecessary tragedy. City authorities had failed to take action upon the recommendations of the Fire Department for increased water pressure, underground power lines in the business district, and removal of large accumulations of trash from various businesses. The disaster ruined one of Augusta's finest residential neighborhoods; many of those who lost their homes forsook the downtown area and chose to build on "the Hill." During its two centuries of existence, Broad Street has suffered several serious fires. On April 3, 1829, the city was being battered by heavy winds similar to the conditions in 1916 when a fire broke out on Broad near Center (5th) Street. In the next few hours, the City Market and many homes

[41]

MANY RESIDENCES along Hawks Gulley were destroyed in the 1908 disaster. Augustans gathered to assist the victims and view the wreckage. The chimney of the Old Powder Works can be seen in the background. (Anderson)

CLEANING UP after the water had receded was a sanitary as well as economic necessity. The Augusta Fire Department pumped out water standing in cellars, and county health officials vaccinated people and advised businessmen and residents of the most effective cleansing and disinfecting techniques. Pictured clearing away the mud and trash at Von Kamp, Vaughan and Gerald Gerald Dry Goods and Notions at the corner of Broad and Jackson were left to right: A. B. Von Kamp, A. J. Montgomery, Willie Lotz, Ashby Mathews, T. J. Vaughan, S. Crawford, and B. Duren. (Anderson)

WHEN HIS CAR STALLED in the 700 block of Greene Street, the driver worked frantically to get it moving before the water rose higher or the current became swifter. (Anderson)

THE FLOODED STREET at the corner of Greene and McKinne (Thirteenth) streets was passable on horseback in 1912. Although water lapped at the steps leading to the Greene Street Presbyterian Church in the background, the building was not damaged. (Thomas)

THE FIRE of 1916 ruined the Dyer Building on the northwest corner of Broad and Jackson (Eighth) streets. Only chimneys and some outer wall remained on March 23, 1916. (RCHS)

east of Center were enveloped in flames, and the wind blew burning debris three and four blocks from the main blaze where more fires broke out. Losses were estimated at $1,000,000.

Another disaster occurred in 1899, when the south side of Broad Street from the Monument east to McIntosh (7th) Street went up in flames. Six months later the west end of the 700 block burned. These two tragedies accounted for damages of over $1,500,000.

In November 1921, fire again struck the south side of Broad on the 700 block. The Harison Building, J. B. White, the *Chronicle,* the Albion Hotel, and the Stag were among the victims of the blaze that engulfed the buildings from Broad to Ellis streets and from the Monument to Jackson (8th) Street.

In reviewing the contemporary accounts of each disaster, the courageous spirit of the people consistently surfaced and was a major factor in restoring the city. Articles in newspapers published throughout the country commented upon this community attitude which was called variously "pluck," "grit," "determined," and "noble."

DYNAMITE HAD TO BE used to stop the spread of the 1916 fire, and to level gutted buildings later on the southeast corner of Washington (Sixth) and Reynolds streets. Not only did the fire destroy many buildings, but it ruined the fine trees growing along Reynolds, Broad, and Greene streets. (RCHS)

FOLLOWING THE FIRE in 1916, outdoor worship services were held behind the ruins of Saint Paul's Church. While the loss to the city in many areas was great, from a sentimental view the burning of the historic Saint Paul's Church was considered the greatest loss sustained by the city. (St. Paul's)

[44]

A TIME TO REPLANT as well as to rebuild came after the fire. Saint Paul's choir posed for a photograph before taking part in the tree planting ceremony. The levee and railroad bridge to North Augusta can be seen in the background. (St. Paul's)

THE CHRONICLE BUILDING had been built only a couple of years earlier as a fire proof structure. As a result, the 1916 fire gutted the interior. but the walls remained standing. When rebuilt as the Marion Building, it became one of Augusta's primary office buildings and still houses professional offices. (McKenzie)

FIRE AGAIN STRUCK the downtown area, and on November 26, 1921, much of the 700 block from Broad through to Ellis streets was a flame. From the Broad Street view, fire hoses can be seen wetting down the smoldering ruins. Soon thereafter, Albion Avenue was cut through the middle of the 700 block from Broad Street to Ellis. (Anderson)

GREENE STREET in 1900 was a boulevard of magnificent homes. Here, two men walking a dog stroll from the direction of Center (Fifth) Street. This block suffered during the fire, flood, and finally the ravages of a superhighway. (APL)

[46]

THE FIRST CHRISITAN CHURCH was located on the northeast corner of Greene and McIntosh (Seventh) streets. Mrs. Emily Tubman, philanthropist, emanicapator, and business woman of the mid-nineteenth century, provided funds to construct the building. When this photograph was taken in 1902, the First Christian Church was situated in an area that was still predominantly residential. (AC)

People, Places, and Progress:
1900 to 1920

AT THE BEGINNING of the twentieth century, Augusta's cotton trade had grown to such a point that the city was known as one of the greatest inland cotton markets in the world. Only Memphis shipped a larger volume east of the Mississippi. Almost a decade would pass before there was any noticeable change in the day-to-day life of the city's citizens.

Fortunately, all the events of this period were not tragedies. In 1911 and 1912, three suburbs—Summerville, Harrisonville, and Nellieville—were annexed to Augusta, increasing the population by nearly 10,000 residents. Expansion was not limited to the city's boundaries and statistics. Augusta already was developing a medical center which in later decades would become one of the finest in the southeastern region. In 1911, the Medical College moved to Railroad Avenue and Harper Street, and shortly thereafter was ranked as a Class A institution by the American Medical Association. At that time few southern schools held this distinction. The University Hospital, adjacent to the Medical College, opened in 1914 and these two facilities formed the nucleus for the future medical complex that by the 1970s encompassed hundreds of acres.

Evidence of Augusta's growth and prosperity also can be seen in the amount of construction completed, underway, and contemplated in 1914 and 1915, the two years prior to the "Great Fire." In addition to the new medical center, the ten-story Chronicle Building, St. Joseph's Academy, the Sixth Ward Fire House, and the Butt Memorial Bridge spanning the canal were completed. The Post Office Building at the Plaza, and the Mary Warren Home for the Aged on Central Avenue still were under construction. Even before the fire, the Richmond County Board of Education had purchased the former

[47]

site of the Schuetzenplatz and planned to erect a new Tubman High School for girls.

To further increase Augusta's economic growth, the city fathers promoted the use of the Savannah for freight transportation. The Augusta-Savannah Navigation Company acquired two steel barges to carry cotton and local products to terminals in Savannah for transfer elsewhere. It was hoped that this competition with the railroads would assure Augusta merchants and manufacturers of the lowest freight rates possible. Despite periodic attempts, use of the river for transportation has never reached its potential.

Toward the end of this period, the United States entered World War I, and Augusta became a bustling town of soldiers when the new military cantonment, Camp Hancock, opened in 1917. Many of the young men who came to the camp for basic training died in the influenza epidemic which reached drastic proportions throughout the nation. To halt the spread of the disease, health officials recommended precautionary procedures and advised against public assemblies. Local volunteers assisted the physicians, nurses, and Red Cross workers in caring for the stricken soldiers and civilians.

In spite of floods, fire and epidemic, the city moved into a new era by the end of the decade. A number of projects were begun which would ensure the future of the city. Civic leaders sponsored a city-wide sewer system, built additional fire stations, repaved the main streets, completed a new water works department, and beautified the area with a number of parks. With a population that had increased as the result of both natural growth and annexation, Augusta showed signs of going forward as the Garden City of the South, and one of the leading trade centers of Georgia and region.

[48]

HACKS line up facing the Monument on Broad Street in 1902. The extent and potential danger of exposed power lines became a serious concern of the Augusta Fire Department. (RCHS)

MR. JULES GODIN and Dr. Henry Godin pose at the door of the Spectacle Company and Jewelry store they operated at 956 Broad Street. Dr. Godin operated his practice at this location until he retired in the early 1960s. (Godin)

JAMES P. RICHARDS' STABLES at 720-24 Ellis Street provided full livery service at the turn of the century. (AC)

A FAVORITE PASTIME at the beginning of the new century was boating on Lake Olmstead. For special occasions, such as this regatta in 1906, Augustans decorated their boats with flowers. (Sheehan)

McGREGOR HALL was erected as the administration building for Haines Institute in 1906. The institute, founded in 1889 by Lucy Laney, was located in the 1300 block of Gwinnett Street, now Laney-Walker Boulevard, and the present site of Lucy Laney High School. In establishing the all-black institution which offered four years of high school and one year of college work, "Miss Lucy," as she was respectfully called, believed that education was a right of all people and a key to a better life for black youths. Lucy Laney herself was the daughter of a slave who became a Presbyterian minister. When she died in 1933, she was buried at the school entrance. Two years later the graduating class erected a monument over her grave. (RCHS)

MAY PARK at the turn of the twentieth century contained a variety of flower beds, tree lined paths, and a pond. The house seen in the right background still stands at the corner of Fenwick and Elbert (Fourteenth) streets. In later years, May Park became a popular playground and recreational area for young people of Pinch-Gut. According to legend, P. G., as the neighborhood generally is known, gained its name as a result of the 1888 flood during which the people living in the extreme eastern portion of the city were marooned for several days. As the water receded and emergency provisions were brought into the area, a Jewish peddler viewing the residents waiting for food supplies commented, "Oh my, look at those pinched guts." (AC)

A DAY'S OUTING at Schuetzenplatz was a great pastime for Augustans. Located off Walton Way, the German Club provided picnic areas there and had a dance hall situated among the trees decorated with multicolored lanterns. The Sheehan family was one of the many Augusta groups to hold their summer gatherings at Schuetzenplatz. (Sheehan)

THE STAFF of the newsroom of the *Augusta Chronicle* stopped the presses in 1908 to pose for the group shot. Left to right: W. B. Seabrook; Grover Hixon; John Sanders (barefoot office boy); James J. Farrell, the *Chronicle* news editor; Arthur Farrell, E. W. Smith; and J. Marvin Haynie, the city editor. The newspaper office, located at 731 Broad Street, later moved to McIntosh (Seventh) Street and back to Broad Street when both the *Chronicle* and *Herald* came under the same management. The *Augusta Chronicle,* the South's oldest newspaper, began in 1785 as the *Augusta Gazette.* (RCHS)

WILLIAM HOWARD TAFT and his family posed on January 24, 1909, at his winter home. The home, located at the end of Cumming Road at Milledge Road, was torn down when Cumming was extended east to Hickman Road. During the winter of 1908-1909, following his election as president, Taft selected his cabinet while vacationing in Augusta. He subsequently came to Augusta on several visits. (RCHS)

A LOCAL DOG SHOW was an occasion for Augustans to socialize and display the latest fashions as well as an opportunity to enter their animals in competition. (Sheehan)

THE CADET at the Academy in 1917 still wore a uniform reminiscent of the Civil War. The young man stands at attention on the grounds of the Court House. In the background is the Signers' Monument dedicated on July 4, 1848, in memory of Georgia's signers of the Declaration of Independence. Lyman Hall and George Walton were reinterred here, but the grave of the third signer, Button Gwinnett, was never located. (AC)

THE BUILDING on the southeast corner of Broad and Campbell (Ninth) streets which housed the Strand Millinery Shop and the U. S. Woolen Mills Company still had the double chimney typical of many nineteenth-century structures. (Anderson)

SIBLEY MANUFACTURING COMPANY, one of Augusta's largest textile mills, derived its power from the Augusta Canal. The large chimney in front of the building is all that remains of the Confederate Powder Mill which supplied the Confederate armies during the Civil War. The Sibley Mill owned fifty acres of nearby land upon which the company operated tenements for the workers. (RCHS)

[54]

BROAD STREET at the Campbell (Ninth) Street intersection looking southwest offered the shopper a variety of selections—a "painless dentist," a snack at the Imperial Cafe, tobacco at the confectionery, or a trim at the barber shop. (Anderson)

COTTON PRODUCTION was not the
only use for local soil. Following the fall
harvest, hay stacks dotted the country-
side. Truck farms, cattle, orchards, and
nurseries were also part of the local
economy. (RCHS)

THE BEGINNINGS OF FARM MECHANIZATION
allowed much more land to be cultivated, but the
human element—the laborer—was still essential for
successful farming. This early reaper was a sharp
contrast to the mule-drawn plow. (RCHS)

A SUNDAY SCHOOL PARADE marched along
Broad Street. Young flower girls dressed in white
flank the men carrying religious banners. Parades,
so much a part of the community life then, became
less and less frequent after the Second World War.
(AC)

LENWOOD HOSPITAL, a Veterans Administration psychiatric-care center, became a unit of the government's hospital services in 1921, but its clinical facilities, designed to care for 1,000 patients, were not fully operational until 1932. The site originally was Saint Joseph's Academy and Convent. When the nuns moved to another area of the Hill in 1916, the building briefly was a resort hotel; then during the war years, the federal government used it as a quarters for the officers stationed at nearby Camp Hancock. The Lenwood's administrative offices now are housed in the original building. (RCHS)

EXERCISE AND SPORTS at Tubman High were considered necessary for good health and self-discipline. Mary Sherman, wearing her Tubman jersey and bloomers, and a classmate posed beside the old school building on Reynolds Street. (Harrison)

THE FEAST OF CORPUS CHRISTI (Body of Christ) was celebrated on the grounds of Saint Mary's Academy at Telfair and McIntosh (Seventh) streets in the 1910s. Each year the Roman Catholics of the city congregated, first in the academy's yard for benediction, then they marched in procession to the grounds of the Christian Brothers' School next door for a second service, and finally proceeded to Saint Patrick's Church on the corner of Telfiar and Jackson (Eighth) streets for the closing ceremony. (Callahan)

JUDGE WILLIAM F. EVE'S HOUSE stood on Troupe Street between Richmond Avenue and Wrightsboro Road. Children enjoy shade of the young trees in front of this late Victorian house. The large front verandas were typical of structures of this period. (RCHS)

THE TUTTLE NEWTON HOME, originally known as the Augusta Orphan Asylum, was chartered in 1852. When Isaac S. Tuttle died in 1855, he left a large financial settlement and his home on Walker and Center (Fifth) streets to the organization. The remainder of his estate passed to the orphanage upon the death of Mr. Tuttle's stepson, Dr. George M. Newton, in 1859. In 1873, it was moved to the corner of Railroad Avenue and Harper Street. A fire destroyed the original home in 1889, but the board of directors erected the Victorian-Gothic structure the next year. In 1911, the building was leased to the Medical College, and ultimately served as the college's administrative offices until it was demolished in the 1950s. The Tuttle Newton Home changed locations several times after leaving the Railroad Avenue site, and is currently located at 2126 Central Avenue. (RCHS)

[57]

WILLIAM M. DUNBAR, mayor of Augusta from 1907 to 1910, checked the morning's mail in his City Hall office with the customary roll-top desk and spittoon. (AC)

THE J. FERDINAND MARSCHALK family and their 1910 Wescott automobile which sold for $2,100 at Edenfield Motors: This photo was taken south of Augusta on Butler's Creek Hill, the scene of many auto wrecks. (Marschalk)

[58]

THE CIRCUS came to town in 1901! Performers and animals marched up Broad Street drawing crowds of enthusiastic spectators who followed them on to the circus grounds for the tent raising. The Commercial Club in the 700 block of Broad can be seen in the center background. (AC)

T. HARRY GARRETT, Augusta educator and principal of Tubman High School from 1903 until he retired in 1945, enjoys the sun at the old Tubman School in 1912. (AC)

TUBMAN HIGH SCHOOL had its beginning in 1874. Mrs. Emily Tubman purchased the building at 711 Reynolds from the Christian Church and established a public school for Augusta's young women. Although a Catholic academy for girls had been in operation for twenty years, the free educational opportunity for girls had been a small school taught by Ben Neely in rented rooms on Broad Street. The class of 1912 gathered at the windows and along the wall for this snapshot taken during recess. (AC)

MIDDY BLOUSES and hair ribbons for the young ladies, starched collars and jackets for the gentlemen, and large, elegant hats for the chaperones were the fashions of the day at this outing of Tubman girls and their beaux in 1912. (AC)

[59]

FAIRS ARE FUN for people of all ages but, for children, the crowds, performers, animals, rides, lights, sounds, and smells create a special fantasy land. Anna Sheehan, Martha D'Antignac, John Sheehan, and Harris D'Antignac paused from a tour of the fair grounds to have their picture snapped. (Sheehan)

THE OLD MONTE SANO SCHOOL was on the corner of Meigs Street and Richmond Avenue. The red wooden building had a large, round hall into which all of the classrooms opened, a centralized design unusual for that time. First-graders in 1914 pictured on the front steps with their teacher, Ida Morris, were (front row, left to right): Adriene Morris, Pearl, Hackett, Dorothy Hill, Mary Harris, Doris Langley, Minnie Tommins, Marian Cullie, and an unidentified visitor. In the back row from left to right: Eugene Marks, an unknown, Harry Glover, Marion Chapman, Sam Fortson, Russell Wright, an unknown, and Charles Griffin. (Tommins)

THE UNIVERSITY HOSPITAL, completed in 1914, was designed by G. Lloyd Preacher at an approximate cost of $500,000. Originally, the 275-bed hospital had three connecting wings. The Barrett wing, on the right, was used for white patients. The Lamar wing, on the left, was used for black patients, and the administrative offices were located in the center section. Upon completion of the new University Hospital in December 1970, this building was sold to the Medical College of Georgia. (RCHS)

THE HENRY BIBLE CLASS gathered in front of Saint John Methodist Church on Greene Street in 1913. This class was chartered by six men on March 8, 1906, and grew to a peak membership of over two hundred members during the 1940s. Still in existence, the Henry Bible Class celebrated its seventieth anniversary in March 1976. In this picture are : 1. Marion Boyd; 2. Frank Harwood; 3. L. B. Cross; 4. Will Love; 5. P. W. Moseley; 6. Phelps Miller; 7. Ed B. Martin; 8. F. L. Wood; 9. J. E. Robinson; 10. W. P. Manning; 11. Dr. C. F. Edwards; 12. Ben Bussey; 13. D. S. P. Wiggins; 14. Prof. C. T. Sego; 15. Dr. R. L. Henry; 16. J. J. Bazemore; 17. H. D. Morris; 18. C. F. McIntosh; 19. Dr. W. Ed Clark; 20. R. W. Wynn; 21 Ben F. Barksdale; 22. C. F. Benson; 23. G. C. Maxwell; 24. J. D. Greene; 25. C. L. Ware; 26. Fred W. Schlein; 27. H. H. Moss; 28. J. W. Corbett; 29. J. W. Beasley; 30. W. A. Miller; 31. C. B. Avary; 32. B. H. Baker; 33. E. W. P. Bond; 34. J. L. Pate; 35. C. E. Brush; 36. R. J. Maxwell; 37. E. L. Burnham; 38. T. J. Gwin; 39. D. H. Eubanks; 40. Robert Kerr; 41. M. E. Beckum; 42. Oswood Yopp; 43. John W. Rheney; 44. F. C. Sego; 45. J. Q. Griffeth, Jr.; 46. L. L. Magruder; 47. L. R. Allen; 48. M. D. Williams, Jr.; 49. J. G. Bailie; 50. E. B. Merry; 51. W. T. Toole. (Craven)

THE BUTT MEMORIAL BRIDGE at Green and Fifteenth streets over the Augusta Canal was named for Augusta native Maj. Archibald Butt, who was a hero of the *Titanic* disaster. He saved many lives before he went down with the "unsinkable" ship. At the time of his death, Major Butt was aide of Pres. William Howard Taft and was returning from a special presidential assignment. (RCHS)

THE WILHENFORD HOSPITAL for children, incorporated in 1900, opened its doors in 1910 at 1436 Harper Street. Funds for the facility were provided by Mrs. William Henry Duff, who along with her late husband had spent several winters at the Bon Air Hotel. Mrs. Duff wished to build a memorial to him and felt the Children's Hospital would be suitable. Her contribution of $25,000 enabled the hospital to be built at the site of the new medical center planned for the Medical College and City Hospital. In naming the hospital, Mrs. Duff took one syllable each from the name of her father William, her husband Henry, and her son Bradford, calling the hospital Wilhenford, with the accent on the second syllable. The hospital served for a half century until expansion of other medical facilities made it obsolete. (RCHS)

THE CELTIC CROSS, erected by the Colonial Dames in Saint Paul's churchyard, marks the site of Fort Augusta, around which the town was settled. This was also the site of Fort Cornwallis, the British fortification during the siege of Augusta in 1781. The cross is surrounded by dogwood and pine trees waiting to be planted as replacements for the trees and shrubs destroyed in the 1916 fire. (St. Paul's)

THE SPRING FESTIVAL at Monte Sano School was directed each year by Mrs. Henri Price, who for half a century was Augusta's most-renowned teacher of dancing, gymnastics, team sports, and social graces. In 1918, students danced around the May Pole as part of the school production, which was held at the Gwin Nixon home at 1007 Hickman Road. (Tommins)

[63]

THE DEDICATION of the new Saint Paul's Church in 1918 was a happy occasion for Augustans of all faiths who hold a special interest and concern for the first parish established in the one-time frontier town. (St. Paul's)

DURING WORLD WAR I, Camp Hancock encompassed the Wrightsboro Road area west of the present Lenwood Hospital. Many of the troops stationed here were from Pennsylvania and Ohio. After the war, a large portion of the camp site became a residential area; Pennsylvania and Ohio avenues were named after those fine young men. An artillery division of 4,500 men trained in the use and movement of field guns *(above)*, while a medical unit *(below)* drilled in the daily routine of setting up a field hospital, and practiced carrying wounded to the rear. At one time, over forty thousand men were stationed in the "tent city." (Pfadenhauer)

A WORLD WAR I BILLBOARD was erected in Barrett Plaza across from the Union Station asking both Augustans and travelers to aid the war effort by not wasting food. (AC)

AUGUSTA JEWISH AND CHRISTIAN LADIES organized a volunteer service agency during World War I. The ladies met the troop trains to hand out coffee and snacks, were social-service aides at Camp Hancock Medical Unit, assisted soldiers and their families during wartime, and served in whatever capacity that they were asked to participate. Members posing here were, front row, left to right: Mrs. Joseph O'Dowd, unknown, Mrs. Herbert Elliott, Mrs. Joseph Mullarkey, Mrs. Charles Sylvester, Mrs. John P. Mulherin, Mrs. Frank Fleming, Mrs. William Mulherin, Mrs. Benedict Goldberg, Mrs. Tom Loyless, Mrs. J. Willie Levy, Mrs.__Jackson, Mrs. Remer Brown, and Mrs. I. B. C. Levy. Back row, left to right: Mrs. Jules Heyman, Mrs.__Oakman, Mrs. Arthur DeVaughn, Mrs. Victor Dorr, Mrs. T. D. Murphy, Miss Blanche Strassberger, Mrs. G. Worth Andrews, Mrs. Joseph L. Mulherin, unknown, Mrs. Clara D. Kinchley, Mrs. Charles Hayes, and Mrs. Stewart Dempsey. (Mulherin)

[65]

COMPANY B of the Military Department of the Academy of Richmond County stands at parade rest beside the old Medical College Building. The cadets are dressed in the summer uniform, worn from April to June, which consisted of khaki breeches, shirt, cap, and leggings. The academy's first military company was organized in 1882. C. A. Doolittle, who is standing in front, was the captain of the unit in 1918. (RCHS)

THE PLAZA HOTEL, which faced Barrett Plaza, was a favorite with travelers because of its location just across Walker Street from Union Station. The cream-colored structure contrasted strikingly with the surrounding red-brick buildings. (C of C)

CARMICHAEL'S CLUB was a popular place for group outings, and its well-stocked pond yielded sizable catches, as for this group *(left)*. And the Sheehans *(below)* enjoyed a sizable family get-together in 1919 with fishing, swimming, and a Southern pit-cooked barbecue. (Sheehan)

Between the Wars: 1920 to 1940

FOLLOWING WORLD WAR I, an era of peace and tranquility settled upon the city. The population which had grown to 52,548 in 1920 climbed still higher to 65,919 in 1940, making Augusta Georgia's third largest city.

With its mild winters, Augusta had long been a haven for those escaping the snows and freezing temperatures of the northern states. Three presidents—Taft, Harding, and Eisenhower—found the city an ideal vacation spot. The weather, often described as marvelous, was a major factor in bringing thousands of visitors to the city in the 1920s. In promoting tourism, the city fathers boasted that the skies were sunny more than 68% of the time. During this period Augusta had three great resort hotels with nearly one thousand rooms, plus many cottages and private inns. Quite a few of those who first came to visit and stayed in a hotel later bought homes in and around the city.

Numerous attractions were provided for the winter guests, including polo, horseback riding, lawn games, tennis, and hunting. Golf, which was a vital part of the recreational activities for both citizens and guests, reached new highs. When the Forrest Hills-Ricker Hotel was completed in 1927, a fine golf course was featured among the facilities available to the guests. Then, in 1933, an event fraught with future significance occurred, when the Augusta National Golf course, designed by Bobby Jones, was completed. The opening of this club and the ensuing Masters Golf Tournament have done more than anything else to put Augusta on the map.

The development of the city as an educational center received a boost in 1925, when the city passed a bond issue for $400,000 to construct a building for the Academy of Richmond County and the newly authorized Junior College of Augusta. This new two-year college, which forty years later was to become a four-year institution, joined two older institutions, the Medical College of Georgia and Paine College in providing additional higher education facilities to the community.

To many Americans, the term "the thirties" immediately calls to mind the harsh, bleak years of the Depression. Generally, Augusta fared better than many metropolitan areas. While financial institutions failed throughout the country, several local banks survived to weather other economic crises. To be sure, there were Augusta firms that failed, families that suffered, and many belts that were tightened. But in the broad view, the city was moving forward. In the 1930s, Augusta acquired its first radio station, watched the first Masters, enlarged the University Hospital with the Milton Anthony Wing, initiated airline and air mail service between the city, New York, and Miami, built the lock and dam below the city, and staged a bicentennial pageant to celebrate Augusta's founding. Federal funds aided the larger projects and supported a local Works Progress Administration.

By the end of the thirties, brighter days seemed in the city's future. In 1938, Congress appropriated the first funds for the Clark Hill Dam and ordered the necessary land purchases to proceed. World War II delayed the Clark Hill project, but local enthusiasm for the dam never waned during the war years.

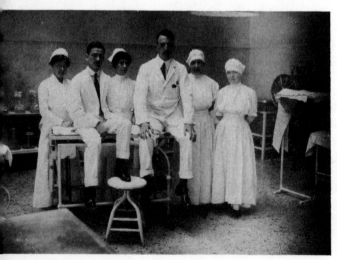

SOME STAFF MEMBERS at University Hospital posed in the operating room in the 1920s. In the post-World War I period, many new medical personnel came to Augusta to work. Miss Alice F. Stewart, supervisor and later director of nurses, is third from the left. (Stewart)

A TREE-TOP VIEW of the city taken after the 1916 fire, looking from the City Hall at Greene and Campbell (Ninth) streets. To the left of the Lamar and Marion buildings, the framework of the Masonic Building can be seen under construction. The building in the left foreground was the Y.M.C.A., which later became the Margaret Hamilton Hotel. (AC)

A TYPICAL SUMMERVILLE COTTAGE built on Battle Row among shade trees and shrubs to take every advantage of the higher, cooler, and supposedly more healthful environment of "the Hill;" A two-story wing has been added on the left to this frame structure that is an example of the Sandhills architecture. (RCHS)

THE AUGUSTA COMMUNITY ORCHESTRA was one of several musical groups in Augusta which included women. This forerunner of the Augusta Symphony Orchestra, assembled for a picture in front of Saint John Methodist Church on Greene Street, used to perform for religious services and special events. (RCHS)

CITY HALL at the corner of Greene and Campbell (Ninth) streets was described in the Federal Writers' Project as "Victorian Gothic with Romanesque influence and a suggestion of the Italian in the red brick and terra cotta ornamentation." Built between 1888 and 1890, it originally housed the post office, until 1916 when the city moved its administrative offices there. It continued as City Hall until the City-County Building was erected in 1957. (C of C)

PRES. WARREN G. HARDING made several visits to Augusta between March 1921 and April 1923. Charles Stulb presented Mrs. Harding with a bouquet of roses on the First Family's departure in April 1923. The last visit was highlighted by a banquet held at the Partridge Inn. Many Augustans enjoyed this opportunity to socialize with one of the chief executives who have been guests in the city. (Stulb)

THE ENTIRE STUDENT BODY of Tubman High School gathered to begin the school year in 1922. The new building, made of cream-colored, pressed brick, opened in February 1918 with 300 girls. Located in the 1700 block of Walton Way, the building was erected on the former site of the Schuetzen-Club. Although the facility was designed for 600 students, the enrollment had mushroomed to 1,200 by 1939. (RCHS)

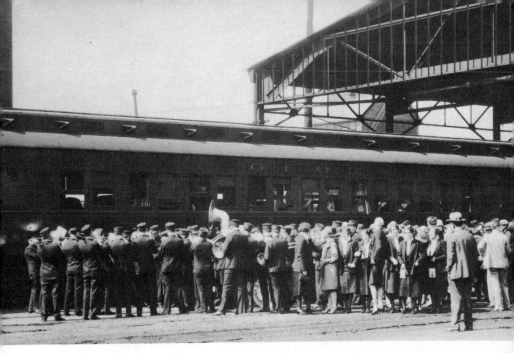

MR. LOUIS SAYRE'S GEORGIA RAILROAD BAND was ready to play at the drop of a hat or the toot of a train whistle. Here he and his group are giving a musical send-off to a convention-bound Augusta association. (AC)

AUGUSTA'S FAMOUS POLICE BAND gathered in front of Police Headquarters on the corner of Campbell (Ninth) and Reynolds streets for the first Police and Firemen's Field Day on September 7, 1925. During the twenties a number of musical groups flourished in Augusta. (RCHS)

THIS COLONIAL EDIFICE stood in 1925 on the southwest corner of Greene and McIntosh (Seventh) streets. Built in the eighteenth century as an inn, the Marquis de la Fayette is supposed to have spoken to the citizens of Augusta from the porch in 1825. In 1930, Dr. Andrew J. Kilpatrick moved the structure to its present location on Pine Needle Road at Comfort Road. (DAR)

THE RICHMOND HOTEL, located across from the Confederate Monument at Albion Avenue in the heart of the downtown area, opened on May 14, 1923, on the site of the old Albion Hotel destroyed by fire in 1921. The new eight-story, 202-room facility, which cost $750,000, was considered the most elegant and complete commercial hotel in the South at that time. Through the years it became especially well known to visiting businessmen and conventioneers. When Pres. Dwight D. Eisenhower vacationed at the Augusta National during his term of office, the Richmond was press headquarters. (C of C)

THE NATIONAL EXCHANGE Bank, incorporated in 1871, was located on the 800 block of Broad Street. In the 1940s, the National Exchange took advantage of its seventy-five years of reliable banking service by advertising, "Old in years and experience, Young in methods and ideas." (C of C)

A VIEW OF BROAD STREET looking west from McIntosh (Seventh) Street, showed the library on the left before it moved to the old Richmond Academy building in 1926. By the mid-1920s, the business sector had recovered from the major fires of 1916 and 1921. (RCHS)

A BOY SCOUT TROOP was sponsored by Saint Patrick's Catholic Church about 1920. The Christian Brother pictured with the scouts taught at the Catholic Boys' School located on Telfair between McIntosh (Seventh) and Jackson (Eighth) streets—the present site of Bell Auditorium. (Callahan)

THE PUMPING STATION on the Augusta Canal was the heart of the operation of this valuable source of water power. Construction on the canal was started in 1845. Because new factories taxed the canal's power, improvements and an enlargement were begun in 1871. (AC)

[73]

MONTROSE was the home of Charles Colock Jones, Jr., from 1877 until his death in 1893. Following graduation from Harvard Law School in 1855, Jones practiced law in his native Savannah. When the Civil War began, he joined the Confederate Army and served as a colonel. For twelve years after the war he conducted his law practice in New York. Then in 1877 he returned to Georgia and made his home at Montrose in the Village of Summerville. Jones was the author of eighty publications including *The History of Georgia* and the *Memorial History of Augusta, Georgia.* Montrose, located at 2249 Walton Way, currently serves as the Fuqua Center for Reid Memorial Presbyterian Church. (RCHS)

[74]

THIS AERIAL VIEW of downtown, looking east, shows the levee that was constructed to hold back the waters of the Savannah River and the road built on top of the bank. In the background is the old Center (Fifth) Street bridge which was partially washed away by the high water in 1929. It was replaced in 1930 by the Jefferson Davis Memorial bridge. (AC)

CLAUSSEN'S BAKERY, one of the Augusta businesses established in the late nineteenth century, became one of the major bakeries in this part of the country. Located for many years in the building at 1589 Broad Street, it became the victim of changing times and closed its doors in the 1960s. (C of C)

ENGINE COMPANY NO. 7 of the Augusta Fire Department is still located at 2163 Central Avenue. The stucco building complemented the houses built on the Hill after the 1916 fire. The fire engine was purchased during the administration of Julian Smith, who was mayor from 1922 to 1925. (C of C)

THE ROTC REGIMENTS of the Academy of Richmond County prepare for a parade as college students watch. The academy moved to the Baker Avenue location in 1926. The Junior College of Augusta, founded by the Board of Education in 1925, began co-educational classes in the new ARC building at the start of the 1926-27 academic year. The academy had been offering fifth-year work since 1910 to students who were able to enter the University of Georgia, Georgia Tech, and several other college as sophomores. (RCHS)

[75]

SAINT MARY'S ACADEMY, conducted by the Sisters of Mercy, was established in 1853 and was located at Telfair and McIntosh streets. Posed in the schoolyard for their 1926 commencement picture were left to right: Louise O'Leary, Kathryn Callahan, Katherine Sherman, Antoinette O'Conner, Margaret Lyons, Anna Hallinan, Sarah Mulherin, Louise Sullivan, and Helen Cashin. (Callahan)

EVERYONE WENT SHOPPING on Broad Street on Saturday. One of the early traffic lights at the intersection of Broad and McIntosh (Seventh) is clearly visible. Traffic, however, was so heavy that the signal light alone could not keep it moving. Three patrolmen stand at various points of the intersection to prevent congestion. Only two lanes of traffic passed along each side of Broad Street until the removal of the streetcar tracks permitted expansion to three lanes, while still retaining center parking. (C of C)

THE 1927 BASKETBALL team at Catholic High School: Run by the Christian Brothers, the school was located on Telfair Street between McIntosh and Jackson streets. Shown here are, bottom row, left to right: Bo Thompson, Bernard Callahan, Andrew Sheehan, Raymond Ward, and Joe Pope. Top row: Robert Arthur, John O'Shea, Robert Leonard, Neil Vaughn, Joe Lyons, and Fritz McCarthy. (Callahan)

MR. CHARLES STULB, SR., one of the city's leading horticulturists and florists, paused briefly while gathering flowers to pose for the photographer. (Stulb)

CHATEAU LeVERT, located on the southwest corner of Bellevue and Arsenal avenues, was one of the homes of Octavia Walton LeVert, the daughter of George Walton and Sarah Walker, and the granddaughter of George Walton, one of the signers of the Declaration of Independence. In 1916, the house became the convent for the sisters of Saint Joseph of Carondolet. When a new home for the nuns was constructed in the 1960s, Chateau LeVert was torn down. (Schweers)

TENNIS was part of the life of leisure at the Forest Hills Hotel. During the twenties and thirties the hotel was one of the leading Southern resorts. (C of C)

WINTER RESIDENTS AND GUESTS took advantage of the warm weather for a round of golf at the Augusta Country Club. The players are, left to right: Mrs. Harold A. Richardson of New York and Augusta, Charles Irvine of Chicago, Mrs. Dorothy C. Hurd of Pittsburgh (a former National Women's Champion), and Col. F. B. Robins of Toronto. (C of C)

THE BON AIR HOTEL was at the height of its popularity as a winter resort. Located on the corner of Walton Way and Hickman Road on the Hill, it had a commanding view of the city. (C of C)

THE PARTRIDGE INN was another major resort in the city. On the Hill on Walton Way opposite the Bon Air Hotel, it is shown here before the balconies were removed. (C ofC)

BOBBY JONES, Augusta's most famous golfer, putts on the ninth green at the Forest Hills Golf Course. After years of exposure to tournament and exhibition play by the world's finest men and women golfers, Augustans have become demanding, "professional" spectators. (C of C)

ED DUDLEY is driving from the first tee in the Southeastern Open Championship at the Forest Hills-Ricker Golf Course in 1930. Later, when the hotel was taken over by the federal government for a hospital, the course became the Armed Forces Golf Course. (C of C)

THE AUGUSTA HORSE SHOW was
considered one of the outstanding social
events of the winter season and gave both
Augustans and members of the "winter
colony" an opportunity to display the
newest fashions *(above)*. But the display
of riding skills was not overlooked either
—Maj. John B. Thompson on Kindred
(right) takes a hurdle in perfect style.
(C of C)

ON THE FOURTH OF JULY in 1929, the kids played on the Court House steps or sat
patiently, waiting for director Louis Sayre to strike up the band. (RCHS)

BRICK MANUFACTURING has been one of the city's leading industries. A spur track was laid near the kilns at Georgia-Carolina Brick Company for ease of loading and transporting the tons of bricks produced at this plant. (C of C)

[82]

THE GEORGIA RAILROAD MACHINE SHOP was a large busy place covering an area bounded by Walker and Fenwick streets on the north and south. With an east boundary on McIntosh (Seventh), the yards extended to the west across Jackson (Eighth) Street. During the Civil War, the Confederacy purchased a locomotive and several freight cars constructed at the Georgia Railroad Shops. Although rail service declined in the post-World War II era, the yard remained a maintenance and repair center until the buildings were torn down in the 1960s. (C of C)

HOLLINGSWORTH CANDY COMPANY
at 827 Telfair Street across from Barrett
Plaza is one of the South's leading manufacturers of fine candy. The company
merged in 1932 with Nunnally Candy
Company of Atlanta to form the present
Fine Products Corporation. The billboard above the plant proudly proclaims
that Hollingsworth's was "the home of
the World's Finest candy," a statement
supported by awards from three French
expositions. (RCHS)

MONTGOMERY WARD and Company
located in the 1100 block of Broad Street
was a leading department store until the
Depression. (C of C)

THE FIRST BAPTIST CHURCH erected this structure on the southwest corner of Greene and Jackson (Eighth) streets in 1902, replacing the 1821 building. During the construction period, the congregation met in the Tubman High School auditorium on Reynolds Street. The church moved from this historic location to Jackson Road and Walton Way in 1975. (C of C)

THE ORIGINAL BUILDING of Saint John Methodist Church, erected in 1801, was sold to the Springfield Baptist Church and moved to the southeast corner of Reynolds and Marbury (Twelfth) streets in 1844. Later the Baptist congregation erected a brick sanctuary facing Marbury, but continues to use the older structure for educational purposes. The Springfield Baptist Church is usually considered the first Baptist Church in America for blacks, having been organized at Silver Bluff, South Carolina, in 1790 and moved to Augusta about 1840. This picture, taken in the early 1930s, also shows a row of the neat frame houses that lined Reynolds Street. (DAR)

THE BASKETBALL TEAM of Haines Institute was champion in 1935. Mr. M. Tutt was director of athletics. (Richardson)

THE STUDENT BODY of Haines Institute gathered in front of Marshall Hall for a group picture in 1935. This was the first building erected at the school, and housed the girls' dormitory and library. (Richardson)

THE AUGUSTA GUN CLUB provided target practice for amateurs as well as sharpshooters. There was no sex discrimination here—women took their turns alongside the men. (C of C)

MILL WORKERS POSE in this interior shot of Sibley Mills. In this area, where the cotton cloth was folded for packing, the clean, light and airy environment pointed up the concern expressed by the company officials for the well-being of its employes. (C of C)

THE GEORGIA RAILROAD and Banking Company, chartered in 1833, bought land at the northwest corner of Broad and McIntosh (Seventh) streets in 1836 for a building which served as its home until the new high-rise, built across the street on the northeast corner, replaced it in 1967. The structure shown here was completed in 1903, and its architecture was in a dignified, conventional neo-classical style, in keeping with the bank's image. (C of C)

THE LOCK AND DAM was dedicated on June 26, 1937. This $1,473,000-project, located at New Savannah Bluff near Bush Field, was a step towards the development of the river between Augusta and the sea by eliminating the shoals and shallows between the city and the Bluff. To mark the occasion, the riverboat *Wiley Moore,* carried a group of civic leaders downriver to the dam and through the locks. Pouring of the first concrete for the lock and dam system had taken place two years earlier on May 13, 1935, as one of the events of the Augusta Bicentennial celebration. (RCHS)

AUGUSTANS lined the levee bank to view the festivities surrounding the lock and dam dedication. The *Wiley Moore* left the Center (Fifth) Street landing with much cheering from the assembled spectators. Many smaller craft also were on the river that day to join the celebration. (RCHS)

AMONG PASSENGERS of the *Wiley Moore* were W. D. Page, Capt. Wiley Moore, Roy Harris, and John Barnes. From the eighteenth century, the river was an important factor in the development of the city, but in the twentieth century—despite various efforts to rejuvinate river transportation—the traffic on the Savannah diminished. In July 1937, several prominent Augustans went by riverboat to Savannah to consult Army engineers and shippers on river-improvement plans. (RCHS)

HAYGOOD HALL was erected on the Paine College Campus in 1897-1899, soon after the property on Fifteenth Street between Gwinnett Street and Central Avenue was acquired. When the picture was taken in 1937, the four-story structure was the main classroom and office building for the college. The clock tower was an Augusta landmark until it was destroyed by fire in 1968. Paine Institute was founded in 1882 by the two branches of Methodism in the South to provide for the education of future black leaders. In 1903, the institution was rechartered as Paine College. (Richardson)

BEHIND THOSE MASKS were a couple of Fourth-of-July celebrants—not Halloween trick-or-treaters. They were just two of the "fantastics" who roamed Augusta's streets on the Fourth.

"Fantastics" wore masks, called "dough faces," and misfit clothing, often with an enormous pillow-stuffed bosom or rear. Almost everyone of them carried a stout stick with which to threaten anyone who bothered him or her. Of course, no one seriously did, for it was all in the spirit of fun. Since the 1830s, "fantastics" were as much a trademark of Augusta as the Confederate Monument. For nearly a century, Augusta was on record as the only city that had this peculiar custom; then Savannah youth began to copy their Augusta friends. By the early 1950s, however, "fantastics" were becoming a rarity on the Fourth. (Callahan)

THE CITIZENS AND SOUTHERN BANK in the 700 block of Broad Street has now expanded eastward to occupy the remainder of the block. By the 1970s, the Georgia Railroad Bank had moved across Seventh Street to a new high-rise structure. The Herald Building shown on the left still houses the daily newspapers. (C of C)

THE 1937 GRADUATING CLASS of University Hospital's
School of Nursing posed at the Doughty Nurses' Home on
Harper Street. From its founding in 1893, the school has provided graduates who have served faithfully in all types of
medical situations—daily routine, nursing care, emergency
cases, disaster, and four wars. (Stewart)

BOBBY JONES and Wendell P. Miller, a New York engineer,
look over blueprints at the site of the "perfect" golf course
in the process of construction in 1933. The new course,
which was built on the site of the Berckmans Estates, was
sponsored by the Augusta National Golf Club, and became
the home of the world-famous Masters. (C of C)

THE GALLERY at the Augusta Country Club watches as
Eugene Homans, Helen Hicks, Maureen Orcutt, and Bobby
Jones play a charity match. Jones and Orcutt won 2-1. Miss
Hicks was a National Women's Champion, and Miss Orcutt
had won the Canadian Women's Championship. (C of C)

THE RICHMOND COUNTY COURTHOUSE, one of the city's oldest structures in the 1930s, originally was constructed as the Augusta City Hall in 1820. The wings were added during remodeling in 1892. In 1916, the City Hall moved to Greene and Campbell (Ninth) streets, and this building continued as the County Court House. The building was torn down in 1957 and replaced by the Augusta-Richmond County Municipal Building. (C of C)

[91]

THE INTERIOR of Dr. Everard Wilcox's Glenn Avenue home shows a transitional-style parlor in the late 1930s. The furniture is a mixture of Empire, Victorian, and comfortable rockers. The pier mirror is the type which may have stood in an older house downtown. (RCHS)

BUSH FIELD in 1941 was a repair and maintenance base for the Army Air Corps. Once the United States entered the war, operations at Bush Field were stepped up drastically. (C of C)

AUGUSTA'S FIRST AIRPORT, Daniel Field, opened in 1927. During World War II, it became an aviation training school. Several of the crews that later bombed Japan attended classes here. The hangars shown in the background were situated where Daniel Village Shopping Center now stands. Oliver General Hospital can be seen at the left of the picture. (C of C)

Boom to Bomb: 1940 to 1950s

THE EVENTS leading to World War II had their effects on Augusta even before Pearl Harbor. While the world powers talked of peace, the Department of the Army was acquiring 56,000 acres on the outskirts of the city in Richmond and surrounding counties. Construction, which began with a large local labor force, was completed in December, 1941, and Camp Gordon was ready for new recruits just a few days after the Japanese attack. Here the Fourth, Tenth, and Twenty-sixth Armored divisions trained for overseas.

The impact of the war and its huge military installation were evident everywhere in the city. The federal payroll which eventually totaled more than $42,000,000 annually produced a prosperity greater than any that the city fathers could have imagined.

From its inception Augusta had been a military town, yet the enormous influx of soldiers, dependents, and transients temporarily stunned this quiet river city. Reacting as they do to emergency situations, however, the people of the community displayed a spirit of cooperation and camaraderie seldom shown under normal conditions. The U. S. O., Red Cross, church and local service clubs did their part for the soldiers away from home. Many of these servicemen fell in love with the city and returned after the war to marry local girls and make Augusta their home.

As the war ended it seemed as if Augusta were headed for a decline. In June 1945, the first G. I.'s were separated from the Army at Camp Gordon, and the importance of the Army in the community appeared almost at an end. New life came to the camp in 1948, however, when the Army moved the Signal Training Center and the Military Police School to Augusta.

On the local political scene, the decisive defeat of the Cracker Party in the election of April 16, 1946, rocked the foundations of the City Hall and Court

House and brought new participants into Augusta government. The party had dominated political power in the city and county for some thirty years. Under the leadership of John Butler Kennedy, the Cracker Party controlled the city government and all civil service, police and fire department appointments. Kennedy ran his power base first from the fire department and later as the Commissioner of Public Safety, a political job created especially for him.

With a forceful Chamber of Commerce at work a number of businesses, industrial firms, and federal projects were attracted to the area. On November 28, 1948, the first contract was awarded to construct the Clark Hill Reservoir which was the culmination of the dreams of two Augustans, Lester Moody, Executive Secretary of the Chamber of Commerce, and former Mayor and *Chronicle* Editor Thomas J. Hamilton. When completed, the dam brought additional electrical power to Augusta, increased flood control, and created one of the largest man-made lakes in the world. The lake and its surrounding area have become one of the most popular recreational areas in the South.

Nothing so elated the local civic and financial interests as did the announcement on November 29, 1950, that a $260,000,000 "Bomb Plant" would be constructed across the Savannah River in Aiken and Barnwell counties, South Carolina. The impact of the development of the E. I. du Pont de Nemours Company, Savannah River Plant, was tremendous. While the 50,000 workers boosted the population and payrolls in the city and surrounding communities, the boom town atmosphere brought problems created by the construction crews. To house the flood of workers, thousands of trailers were brought in, and temporary cities sprang up overnight. The economic growth begun at this time has continued. However, prosperity did not touch everyone's life. Problems of housing, unemployment, and poverty still remained to be solved.

Augusta moved into the second half of the twentieth century with more emphasis than ever on the development of new industries to meet its changing needs. The small Indian trading post was now on the threshold of becoming an urban industrial center.

CONSTRUCTION OF CAMP GORDON began before the nation entered World War II, but in early 1942 there was a tremendous effort to provide adequate housing for the incoming troops. (Pfadenhauer)

AIR CADETS at Daniel Field present the colors during a World War II military ceremony. (AC)

AN ASSEMBLY LINE at the Augusta Arsenal briefly paused for a photograph. During World War II, the labor force and ordnance services reached the highest peak in the history of the arsenal. (Pfadenhauer)

THE AUGUSTA UNIT of the Georgia State Guard had been one of the many units trained to defend the home front during World War I. In 1943, the Augusta unit, 300 strong, left for Camp Rutledge for training. (AC)

THE U.S. ARMY MILITARY POLICE SCHOOL was based at Camp Gordon for over twenty-five years. Soldiers from all over the country were sent to this special school, established here during World War II. (RCHS)

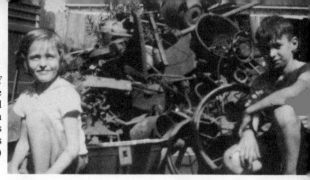

SCRAP-IRON COLLECTION was one of the many ways Augusta's young people participated in the war effort. The local citizens were also asked to save their tin cans, cigarette wrappers, and other items that could be converted into materials of war. (Callahan)

OLIVER GENERAL HOSPITAL was Augusta's second Veterans Administration medical center. By the 1940s, the city's heyday as a resort center had waned, but the facilities were put to good use. The federal government took over the Forest Hills Hotel, converted it into a military hospital, and added miles of connecting annexes for patient bed-care, rehabilitation, and clinics. The former hotel's famous golf course and practice greens offered the opportunity for therapeutic exercise and recreation. The Veterans Administration took over Oliver General Hospital in 1950. (C of C)

THE FIRST GRADE of Monte Sano School gathered in 1941 for the traditional class picture. The school, begun in 1893 with twenty-five students at the rear of the Harper house on Wrightsboro Road, moved into the new brick structure on Richmond Avenue in 1924. Carl Sanders, a former student at Monte Sano, was governor of Georgia from 1963-1967. (Fair)

THE SOCIAL SCIENCE DEPARTMENT was only one part of the fine faculty teaching at Richmond Academy-Junior College in 1942. Members pictured here are, left to right: W. P. Smith, T. J. Huffman, C. G. Cordle, George Howard, and N. L. Galloway. Mr. Cordle and Mr. Galloway joined Junior College of Augusta when that institution moved to a separate campus on the old arsenal grounds. (AC)

THIS AERIAL VIEW of downtown shows the levee and the Savannah River on the right, with the Fifth Street bridge and the railroad bridge in the lower corner, and the North Augusta (Thirteenth Street) Bridge in the upper corner. The distinctive wide span of Broad Street is clearly visible on the left. Trees still lined Broad and Reynolds streets east of Fifth Street in the 1940s. (C of C)

DELTA AIRLINES restored full service to Daniel Field in the postwar period when the city airport returned to its original status, handling both commercial and private planes. The municipal airport moved to Bush Field in the early 1950s, southeast of the city, and Daniel Field became a general aviation airport. (C of C)

UNION STATION, located on the south side of Barrett Plaza at Walker Street, served six railroad lines during the 1940s. During the war years there was heavy traffic through the station as troop trains arrived with recruits to be trained at Camp Gordon and later "pulled out" for embarkation centers for overseas duty. During the summer and fall of 1945, many Augustans met train after train, anxiously searching for returning relatives. (C of C)

THE MARION BUILDING in the 700 block of Broad Street offered convenient office space for the postal telegraph, lawyers, realtors, dentists, doctors, engineers, and various other professional and business firms. Next door, the Imperial Theater, with its penguin-bedecked banner, "It's COOL Inside," tempted summer shoppers to abandon briefly the Broad Street heat. Few Augusta buildings could boast of air conditioning in the 1940s. (C of C)

THE "FORTY AND EIGHT" had a grand time initiating eleven new members in July 1945. The organization is composed of World War vets who perform notable service to the American Legion. Three Richmond County posts and several others from nearby counties comprised the Voiture Locale, which in 1945 had over fifty members. (AC)

THE SAFETY PATROL was a vital part of every school. These boys (girls were included later) assisted the school children to exit the building in an orderly fashion, cross streets safely, and catch the proper buses. The patrol shown here in 1947 were, front row, left to right; unknown, Jody Lee, Ed Riddle, unknown; second row, Scotty Langham, Ham Holland; back row, Breck Brigham, unknown, Skeeter Griffin, Pete Whatley, Sanford Prickett, John Brinson, and Billy Fair. (Fair)

THE AUGUSTA COUNTRY CLUB'S golf course has long held an excellent reputation, and for years was the home of the Titleholders, a national invitational golf tournament for women. This aerial view was taken looking toward the corner of Milledge and Gardner streets, (C of C)

PROFESSOR CHARLES G. CORDLE gives his Junior College history class one of his famous "little quizzes." In this picture, taken at the Academy of Richmond County building in 1945, the classrooms remain as they were when the building was constructed in 1926. Mr. Cordle's career began in 1916 when he joined the faculty of the academy. He retired in 1961 as professor of history at Augusta College. (AC)

[103]

THE SOUTHWEST CORNER of Broad and Campbell (Ninth) streets was one of the busiest places downtown. By the 1940s, Walgreen Drugs had taken over the previous location of Dr. Duncan's Dentist Parlor and the Confectionary. (C of C)

BROAD STREET SHOPPERS crowd the sidewalk as they search the downtown stores for the best bargains. The southeast corner of Broad and Campbell streets was a busy intersection on this particular summer afternoon. Since the 1920s, the Quality Shop, Fifth Avenue Shoppe, and Kinney Shoes had replaced the U.S. Woolen Mills and the Strand Milliners. (C of C)

WHEN SUMMER RESIDENCES were built in Summerville, and later when more families moved to the Hill, many homes had servants' quarters behind the main house. This cottage in back of the Alfred Baker home on Walton Way was remodeled into a modern home for Mr. and Mrs. Thomas Houck. (RCHS)

THE RICHMOND COUNTY Historical
Society held its first dinner meeting on
March 26, 1947, in the Crystal Room at
the Sheraton Bon Air Hotel. The society,
organized in 1946 under the leadership
of Mary Carter Winter, was instrumental
in purchasing the "White House" for preservation. In this picture are James C.
Harrison, Jr., arrangements chairman; Dr.
Fletcher M. Green, professor of history at
the University of North Carolina and
speaker at the dinner; Mrs. Green; Mrs.
Winter, then secretary and later president
of the society; and A. Brian Merry, first
president of the society. (RCHS)

THE "WHITE HOUSE," located at 1822 Broad Street, as it appeared in 1946 when it
was purchased by the Richmond County Historical Society, was in need of extensive re-
pairs. Later, the society deeded the property to the State of Georgia. Following restora-
tion, the state opened the site as the Mackay House on July 15, 1964. It was believed
earlier that the house was the scene of a siege in 1780; new research, however, indicates
that the house was constructed during the postwar period. It remains, nevertheless, an
architectural beauty of the late colonial period. (RCHS)

LAKE OLMSTEAD during the thirties and forties had changed somewhat from its earlier heyday. The pavilion and most of the boathouses had disappeared, but a free swimming area with diving boards, a slide, and a sandy beach still attracted large numbers of Augustans. Julian Smith Park at Lake Olmstead also contained a casino, a barbecue pit, and facilities for outdoor concerts. (C of C)

SWIMMING at Getzen's, across the Savannah in North Augusta, was a favorite pastime for Augustans. Many schools, churches, and clubs held their annual picnics at the pond, which had the added attraction of a large sand pit for sliding and climbimg. (Callahan)

GIRLS' BASKETBALL teams also were a part of the Augusta sports scene in the 1940s. Several of the grammar schools and both girls' high schools boasted well-coached teams. (Callahan)

THE YMCA has sponsored basketball leagues for years as a part of its varied programs to serve Augusta's male population. A "tie-ball" seemed a fair call for this game in the late 1940s. The "Y" at the corner of Broad and Macartan streets has long been a meeting place for ball games, swimming, weight-lifting, boxing, and exercising, as well as a place for quiet reading, chess, and checkers. (Callahan)

ALLEN PARK provided a safe, shady place for a boy to play with his pet goat, The park was a favorite spot for Augustans to stroll, swing, play ball, climb monkey bars, picnic, or just plain relax. There were also annual events such as the Easter Egg Hunt and the city-wide Marble Tournament to be enjoyed. The municipal stadium located at Allen Park was the home of the Augusta Tigers during the 1940s. (C of C)

[107]

JITTERBUG, JAZZ, jive, shag, and the "Big Band" sound were all a part of the postwar period. Augustans took time out for an evening of fun and dancing at a riverboat docked on the Savannah. Charles Fulcher and his orchestra provided the music. (RCHS)

THE AUGUSTA TIGERS, once a New York Yankee farm team, played in the South Atlantic League. During the 1940s, the Municipal Stadium at Allen Park rang with the fans' cheers and jeers during the Tigers' home games. The sports announcer, Thurston Bennett, described the action by radio for home and road games. When the team was doing well, his lively and biased accounts were punctuated with a "Hot-digger-dy-dog!" (C of C)

WIDOWS' HOME CHRISTMAS TEA was looked forward to with anticipation each holiday season. Mrs. Gene Howerdd and Miss Terence Battey were among the hostesses serving the widows at their home in the 200 block of Greene Street. (RCHS)

SCOTT APPLEBY'S home on the corner of Walton Way and Johns Road is a regal example of the Greek Revival manner, its massive Doric columns rising to the roof at back and at front. Known as the Montgomery Place, it was built by Judge Ben Warren in 1830. Later Mr. Appleby gave the house to the city, and it is currently used as a branch of the Augusta Regional Library. During the summer months, concerts are held on the back terrace. (RCHS)

THE GIRL SCOUTS dedicate themselves to God, Country, and Family. Troop 17 celebrated Thanksgiving 1948, by inviting their mothers to a banquet that they had prepared. The scouts standing behind their honored guests were left to right: Betty Dorr, Nellie Callahan, Patricia Hickson, Maxine Jackson, Mrs. Sam Fennell (troop leader), Margarita Fennell, Joanne LeBlanc, Shirley Daniels, Connie LaMontagne, Betty Altoonian, and Melvis Bailey; seated are Mrs. Callahan, Mrs. Hickson, Mrs. Ella Boeckman, Mrs. LeBlanc, Mrs. Daniels, Mrs. LaMontagne, Mrs. Altoonian, and Mrs. Bailey. Mrs. Boeckman, a well-known church and school worker, was a special guest. (Callahan)

MUSIC FOR A DANCE at Boys' Catholic High School was furnished by a phonograph in the late 1940s. Most of the young ladies in attendance were students at the all-girls' school, Mount Saint Joseph. The teenagers shown dancing are, left to right: Joan Sullivan, Pat Carr, Cecilia Roberts, unknown, unknown, Mimi Rice, Neil Callahan, Frankie Kearns, Bernard Mulherin, Dorothy Tobin, and Tommy Reese. (Callahan)

[110]

THE WOMANLESS WEDDING, in which the roles were taken by men instructors of the Academy of Richmond County and the Junior College of Augusta and performed for the benefit of the Parent Teacher Association, was considered one of the funniest events of the late 1940s. Left to right seated are: Wallace Partridge, Mutt Bearden, Eric Hardy; standing, Louis Reese, Frank Inman, Chester Sutton as the groom, J. C. Luckey as the bride, and Guy Hurlbutt as the marrying parson. (AC)

THE "GOLD R" was one of the most-coveted awards at Richmond Academy. Among the qualifications to merit this prize, a student had to maintain an average of 80 for his high-school years and participate actively in various extracurricula functions. The "Gold R" winners in 1949-50 were (front, left to right): Herbert Elliott, Jr., Tommy Herndon, Harry Sherman, Jimmy Pyle; (back row): William H. Evans, Ronald E. Jester, William H. Berry, and Righton Robertson, Jr. (AC)

RICHMOND COUNTY HISTORICAL SOCIETY members enjoyed all the ingredients of a typical Southern picnic in the garden at Appleby Library—Southern-fried chicken, potato salad, beans, tomatoes, rolls, and watermelon. Serving their plates (and sneaking a taste), clockwise around the table, are Mrs. Spencer Hart, Mrs. Richard Torpin, Miss Terence Battey, Mrs. Ruby McCrary Pfadenhauer, Spencer Hart, Mrs. Mary Carter Winter, Dr. Richard Torpin, and Mrs. Louise Barrett. (RCHS)

SACRED HEART CHURCH at Greene and McKinne (Thirteenth) streets was dedicated in 1900. James Cardinal Gibbons was present for the ceremonies. The Jesuit priests completed the original church building in 1874, but the parish soon outgrew that small stucture. Construction on the beautiful brick church began in 1898. Considered one of the region's architectural gems with its stained-glass windows, turrets, arches, unique masonry, and Byzantine dome, Sacred Heart stands in marked contrast to the simplicity of the earlier city church buildings. (RCHS)

THE CLARK HILL DAM project on the Savannah River above Augusta was authorized by the Flood Control Act of 1944. Work on the dam began in 1948 and was completed in 1954 at an estimated cost of $86,000,000. The reservoir provided not only flood protection for the surrounding counties but also created a major recreation area. (C of C)

A FULL-SIZED REPLICA of the Liberty Bell was used in May 1950 to kick off a U.S. Savings Bond drive. Augusta civic leaders and the Girl Scouts joined in a bell-ringing ceremony at the corner of Broad and McIntosh (Seventh) streets. (RCHS)

THE OLIVER GENERAL HOSPITAL was the scene of a hearing of a subcommittee of the U.S. House of Representatives Military Affairs Committee in March 1950. The government was considering closing the hospital since the Veterans Administration opposed assuming the task of operating it. Local civic leaders persuaded Congressman Mendell Rivers of South Carolina (standing) to bring the subcommittee for an inspection of OGH and to hear testimony in support of retaining the Augusta medical-care facility. The efforts to save the hospital were successful, and the VA took it over shortly before the Korean conflict. (C of C)

CUB SCOUTS Den 2, Pack 15, and Den 6, Pack 10, toured the arsenal in the early 1950s. Pictured here with Den 2 Mother, Mrs. L. F. Benson, are Billy Sowers, Art Robinson, Gordon Benson, Eugene Staulcup, Marshall Coursey, Donald Kemp, Billy Dunn, Rosa Benson, and Jaymee Sowers, all of Den 2; and Billy Carpenter, Wilson Folk, Kerk Rankan, Dana Nider, Jack Luttes, Phillip Brown, and Jimmy Sturgis, all of Den 6. In the background to the right stands Bellevue Cottage, constructed circa 1805 as the home of Freeman Walker, mayor of Augusta from 1817 to 1819. (Pfadenhauer)

[114]

THE AMERICAN RED CROSS sponsored a "talking-letters" project during the Korean War to keep Augusta servicemen in touch with their relatives and informed of family and local events. Mrs. C. A. Callahan recorded a letter to her son Neil. (Callahan)

THE LAWN OF OLIVER GENERAL HOSPITAL was the scene of many band concerts and picnics for patients during the Korean War. Hospital personnel, volunteers, and visitors—especially the children—helped bring a touch of home to the servicemen. (C of C)

THE CHINESE SUNDAY SCHOOL of the First Baptist Church was organized in November 1885 by Mrs. A. Smith Irvine and Mrs. Isabella Jordan. Chinese laborers were brought to Augusta to work on improvement of the canal in 1871. After completion of the project in 1875, most of the Chinese workmen decided to stay on. Sending for their families in the 1880s, they have formed the nucleus of the present Chinese community, which today is the second largest Chinese group in the South. (RCHS)

MARDI GRAS festivities in Augusta were on a much smaller scale than those celebrated in some Southern cities, such as New Orleans and Mobile. An important event of the local pre-Lenten activities was the Coronation Ball. In this picture, Queen Anne Marie Weigle holds court while King Phillip Lully looks on; Betsy Ward was the princess, Judy Sommervold and David Claffey the young attendants. (Fair)

THE ARTS have always been an important part of Augusta's multi-faceted life. Local talents are displayed in the Augusta Symphony, Civic Ballet, Augusta Players, Choral Society, recitals, exhibits, poems, novels, and many other creative outlets. Mrs. Elizabeth Wright puts the finishing touches on a portrait. (RCHS)

CARY MIDDLECOFF, a Masters Champion, blasts out of a trap beside the tenth green during the Masters Tournament. (C of C)

THE FORMER HOME of Dr. E. E. Murphy at 432 Telfair Street: Originally constructed around 1801, the building of brick, overlaid with stucco, has been decorated with ornamental ironwork. The wings at each end are later additions. Acquired from the heirs of Dr. Murphy by the Junior League of Augusta, the house is now the headquarters of Historic Augusta. (RCHS)

COTTON REMAINED a key industry for Augusta. Firms dealing with cotton and its by-products still hired the largest percentage of Augusta wage earners, despite the local construction boom in the early 1950s. (C of C)

MAMIE'S CABIN stands nestled among the trees and shrubbery on the grounds of the Augusta National Golf Course. Members of the club approved the construction of the vacation home for President and Mrs. Eisenhower at a cost of more than $100,000. The Eisenhowers first visited Augusta in 1948 so that the then-five-star general could play golf on this famous course. (RCHS)

SISTER ROBERTA JOSEPH SUTTON, Sr. Mary Louise Herman, and Sr. Mary Margaret Toomey surveyed the site of the future St. Joseph's Hospital. Sister Mary Louise, a well-known and highly respected native Augustan, was the capable administrator of the hospital until her death in January 1971. (St. Joseph's Hospital)

ST. JOSEPH'S HOSPITAL was dedicated on December 10, 1952. The hospital operated by the Sisters of Saint Joseph of Carondelet was built through the donations of Augustans of all faiths. Msgr. James J. Grady, a major force in bringing a dream to reality, was photographed as he spoke to the crowd which included civic leaders, religious dignitaries, and local citizens. Music for the occasion was provided by the Camp Gordon Army Band. The hospital, located at the southern end of Winter Street, was enlarged in both the 1960s and 1970s. (St. Joseph's Hospital)

TEEN TOWN, sponsored by the Junior Women's Club, was an administrative as well as recreational experience. The teenagers elected a mayor and a city council to govern their "town," which was located on Central Avenue across from the City Water Works. Dances, shuffleboard, volleyball, ping pong, pool, chess, checkers, and chatter all went into making Teen Town a favorite hang-out during the 1950s. In 1952, William E. Fair succeeded William "Butch" Mulherin, who had been Teen Town's first mayor. Shown hanging the mayor's picture are, left ot right: Mrs. Barbara Weigle, Billy Fair, Billy Watkins, and Miss Ann Hammett. (Weigle)

TEEN TOWNERS handled their own programs from the idea through the planning stages to the cleaning up afterwards. Junior Women's Club volunteers were always present to advise, listen, and lend a hand. Pictured seated with Mrs. Barbara Weigle of the Junior Women's Club in 1953 is Beth Wright, and, standing, are Jennie Lee Lehmann, Barbara Mulherin, and Barbara Bowen. (Weigle)

[119]

THE AMERICAN LEGION Auxiliary sponsored Girls' State, a conference of young ladies from throughout Georgia who met in Atlanta for a week to learn and participate in the day-to-day experience of governing the state. In June 1953, Mrs. Raymond Odum, president of Richmond Post No. 63, and Mrs. C. M. Pelonero, chairman of the local Girls' State project, sent off Augusta's two representatives, Helen Daniels (left) and Helen Callahan (right). (Callahan)

THE MILITARY BALL, which became a celebrated annual event at Richmond Academy, was initiated by the Academy's Sabre Club in 1948. The club was composed of the school's cadet officers who each year chose an honorary cadet colonel from young ladies nominated by the members. In 1954, Honorary Cadet Colonel Katherine Bailey and Cadet Colonel D. Landrum Harrison have the honor and pleasure of the first dance. (Harrison)

THE RICHMOND COUNTY Historical Society emphasizes the collection, preservation, and dissemination of the written history of Augusta and Richmond County. Several of the officers and directors are

pictured at one of the society's two yearly meetings. Standing, left to right, are Lester S. Moody, Joseph B. Cumming, Heard Robertson, Charles G. Cordle, William D. Harden; seated are Mrs. N. H. Gowing, Miss Terence Battey, and Mrs. Lester V. Stone. (AC)

MICKIE GALLAGHER posed with golfers in a Ladies' Day Tournament at the Armed Forces Course in the early 1950s. Gallagher was for many years one of the best known and respected pros in the southeast. (C of C)

THE CONFEDERATE MONUMENT, focal point of Broad Street, was erected by the Ladies' Memorial Association in 1878. The base of the seventy-two-foot monument is granite, and the shaft and fine figures are Carrara marble. The four statues on the first section are generals Robert E. Lee, Stonewall Jackson, Thomas R. R. Cobb, and William Henry Walker. The statue of the private standing at rest atop the column represents all the "men of Richmond County, who died in the Cause of the Confederate States." Berry Benson of Augusta was the model. Gov. Alfred H. Colquitt, a war hero, and Mrs. Andrew Jackson attended the unveiling on October 31, 1878. (C of C)

MILITARY POLICE raise the flag before Post Headquarters at Camp Gordon. The base, which became Fort Gordon in the 1960s, has been a significant influence upon Augusta economically, socially, culturally, and politically. The military has always been an important element in Augusta's history. During each major crisis in our country's history, Augusta has been the site of an important military installation. (C of C)

THE SAVANNAH RIVER PLANT of the Atomic Energy Commission, built in neighboring Aiken County, was a major influence on setting off Augusta's years in the early 1950s. A group of workers were photographed as they leave a wing of one of the two giant hexagonal buildings that housed administrative offices in the 1950s. (C of C)

HIGHWAY EXPANSION was a much-needed project to relieve traffic congestion as Augustans increasingly moved to the suburbs and drove into the city to work and shop. The construction of the new superhighway (U.S. Nos. 1, 78, and 25) cut into the residential area of Center (Fifth) Street; most of the families displaced by the road's progress were relocated in the county. The move of Augustans out of the city continued at an accelerated rate during the next two decades and the enlarged highway system permitted them easy access to the city. (C of C)

THE SIXTEENTH HOLE at the Augusta National has long been a favorite with Masters fans, who have dubbed it, "the water hole," because of the long approach over the pond to the green, and also because a refreshment stand is located nearby. (C of C)

[124]

THE AUGUSTA NATIONAL CLUBHOUSE terrace during the Masters provides members and players a place to relax, have refreshments with family and friends, and to watch the multi-colored outfits of Masters spectators as they pass by. (C of C)

PRES. DWIGHT D. EISENHOWER laid the cornerstone of the new Reid Memorial Presbyterian Church on April 18, 1954. As the President was applying the mortar with an engraved trowel, he remarked, "I used to do this [lay brick] on the farm." Shown watching the President are standing center to right: Joseph Yasney, the Rev. Massey M. Heltzel, pastor, William H. Cooper, and G. E. Cleveland. Charter members present at the ceremony were (seated, front row, left to right), Mrs. Charles M. Mell, Mrs. Walter Percey Danforth, and Mr. Danforth; (back row), Mrs. Sara Mell Seabrook, Mrs. Camilla Danforth, and Mrs. R. P. Richardson. Mr. Wallace Scales is shown behind the charters members. (Reid)

[125]

THE AUGUSTA SYMPHONY, a volunteer group of musicians augmented by professionals from other symphony orchestras, gives a series of orchestral concerts and an operatic production each year. Harry Jacobs directs the Augusta Symphony, which is a source of pride and pleasure to the city. Mr. Jacobs founded the orchestra in 1954. (C of C)

"ALWAYS THE RIVER runs beneath our thoughts. The town is river-born . . .—Always the river." (RCHS)   *Eugene Edmund Murphey*

Index of Names

REFERENCES

FAIR GROUND.

AU